# THE GIANT RAFT.

# THE CRYPTOGRAM.

**BY**

**JULES VERNE.**

Fredonia Books
Amsterdam, The Netherlands

# The Giant Raft
## The Cryptogram

**by**
Jules Verne

ISBN 1-58963-081-5

Fredonia Books
Amsterdam, The Netherlands
http://www.FredoniaBooks.com

# THE CRYPTOGRAM.

*CONTENTS.*

# THE CRYPTOGRAM.

---

## CHAPTER I.

PAGE.
MANAOS - - - - - - - - - 7

## CHAPTER II.
THE FIRST MOMENTS - - - - - - 11

## CHAPTER III.
RETROSPECTIVE - - - - - - - 17

## CHAPTER IV.
MORAL PROOFS - - - - - - - 23

## CHAPTER V.
MATERIAL PROOFS - - - - - - 30

## CHAPTER VI.
THE LAST BLOW - - - - - - 35

## CHAPTER VII.
RESOLUTIONS - - - - - - - 44

## CHAPTER VIII.
THE FIRST SEARCH - - - - - - 49

## CHAPTER IX.
THE SECOND ATTEMPT - - - - - 55

## CHAPTER X.

A CANNON SHOT - - - - - - 59

## CHAPTER XI.

THE CONTENTS OF THE CASE - - - - - 67

## CHAPTER XII.

THE DOCUMENT - - - - - - 72

## CHAPTER XIII.

IS IT A MATTER OF FIGURES? - - - - 81

## CHAPTER XIV.

CHANCE! - - - - - - - 89

## CHAPTER XV.

THE LAST EFFORTS - - - - - - 97

## CHAPTER XVI.

PREPARATIONS - - - - - - 103

## CHAPTER XVII.

THE LAST NIGHT - . - - - - 110

## CHAPTER XVIII.

FRAGOSO - - - - - - - 117

## CHAPTER XIX.

THE CRIME OF TIJUCO - - - - - 123

## CHAPTER XX.

THE LOWER AMAZON - - - - - - 130

# THE GIANT RAFT.

# THE CRYPTOGRAM.

## CHAPTER I.

### MANAOS.

THE town of Manaos is in 30 deg., 8 min., 4 sec. south latitude, and 67 deg., 27 min. west longitude, reckoning from the Paris meridian. It is some 420 leagues from Belem, and about ten miles from the embouchure of the Rio Negro.

Manaos is not built on the Amazon. It is on the left bank of the Rio Negro, the most important and remarkable of all the tributaries of the great artery of Brazil, that the capital of the province, with its picturesque groups of private houses and public buildings, towers above the surrounding plain.

The Rio Negro, which was discovered by the Spaniard Favella in 1645, rises in the very heart of the province of Popayan, on the flanks of the mountains which separate Brazil from New Grenada, and it communicates with the Orinoco by two of its affluents, the Pimichin and the Cassiquary.

After a noble course of some 1700 miles it mingles its cloudy waters with those of the Amazon through a

mouth 1100 feet wide, but such is its vigorous influx
that many a mile has to be completed before those
waters lose their distinctive character. Hereabouts
the ends of both its banks trend off, and form a huge
bay fifteen leagues across, extending to the islands
of Anavilhanas; and in one of its indentations the
port of Manaos is situated. Vessels of all kinds are
there collected in great numbers, some moored in the
stream awaiting a favorable wind, others under repair
up the numerous iguarapes, or canals, which so ca-
priciously intersect the town, and give it its slightly
Dutch appearance.

With the introduction of steam vessels, which is now
rapidly taking place, the trade of Manaos is destined
to increase enormously. Woods used in building and
furniture work, cocoa, caoutchouc, coffee, sarsaparilla,
sugar-canes, indigo, muscado nuts, salt fish, turtle
butter, and other commodities, are brought here from
all parts, down the innumerable streams into the Rio
Negro from the west and north, into the Madeira from
the west and south, and then into the Amazon, and by
it away eastwards to the coast of the Atlantic.

Manaos was formerly called Moura, or Barra de Rio
Negro. From 1757 to 1840 it was only part of the
captaincy which bears the name of the great river at
whose mouth it is placed; but since 1826 it has been
the capital of the large province of Amazones, borrow-
ing its latest name from an Indian tribe which formerly existed in these parts of Equatorial America.

Careless travelers have frequently confounded it
with the famous Manoa, a city of romance, built, it
was reported, near the legendary lake of Parima—
which would seem to be merely the Upper Branco, a
tributary of the Rio Negro. Here was the Empire of
Eldorado, whose monarch, if we are to believe the fa-
bles of the district, was every morning covered with
powder of gold, there being so much of the precious
metal abounding in this privileged locality, that it was
swept up with the very dust of the streets. This as-
sertion, however, when put to the test, was disproved,
and with extreme regret, for the auriferous deposits

which had deceived the greedy scrutiny of the gold-
seekers turned out to be only worthless flakes of mica!

In short, Manaos has none of the fabulous splendors
of the mythical capital of El Dorado. It is an ordinary town of about 5,000 inhabitants, and of these at
least 3,000 are in Government employ. This fact is to be
attributed to the number of its public buildings, which
consist of the Legislative Chamber, the Government
House, the Treasury, the Post-office, and the Custom-
house, and, in addition, a college founded in 1848, and
a hospital erected in 1851. When with these is also
mentioned a cemetery on the south side of a hill, on
which, in 1669, a fortress, which has since been demolished, was thrown up against the pirates of the Amazon, some idea can be gained as to the importance of
the official establishments of the city. Of religious
buildings it would be difficult to find more than two,
the small Church of the Conception and the Chapel
of Notre Dame des Remedes, built on a knoll which
overlooks the town. These are very few for a town
of Spanish origin, though to them should perhaps be
added the Carmelite Convent, burnt down in 1850, of
which only the ruins remain. The population of
Manaos does not exceed the number above given, and
after reckoning the public officials and soldiers, is
principally made up of Portuguese and Indian mer-
chants belonging to the different tribes of the Rio
Negro.

Three principal thoroughfares of considerable ir-
regularity run through the town, and they bear names
highly characteristic of the tone of thought prevalent
in these parts—God-the-Father Street, God-the-Son
Street, and God-the-Holy-Ghost Street!

In the west of the town is a magnificent avenue of
centenarian orange-trees, which were carefully respected by the architects who out of the old city made
the new. Round these principal thoroughfares is in-
terwoven a perfect network of unpaved alleys, inter-
sected every now and then by four canals, which are
occasionally crossed by wooden bridges. In a few
places these iguarapes flow with their brownish

waters through large vacant spaces covered with straggling weeds and flowers of startling hues, and here and there are natural squares shaded by magnificent trees, with an occasional white-barked sumaumeira shooting up, and spreading out its large dome-like parasol above its gnarled branches.

The private houses have to be sought for amongst some hundreds of dwellings of very rudimentary type, some roofed with tiles, others with interlaced branches of the palm-tree, and with prominent miradors, and projecting shops for the most part tenanted by Portuguese traders.

And what manner of people are they who stroll on to the fashionable promenade from the public buildings and private residences? Men of good appearance, with black cloth coats, chimney-pot hats, patent-leather boots, highly-colored gloves, and diamond pins in their necktie bows; and women in loud, imposing toilets, with flounced dresses and headgear of the latest style; and Indians, also on the road to Europeanization in a way which bids fair to destroy every bit of local color in this central portion of the district of the Amazon!

Such is Manaos, which, for the benefit of the reader, it was necessary to sketch. Here the voyage of the giant raft, so tragically interrupted, had just come to a pause in the midst of its long journey, and here will be unfolded the further vicissitudes of the mysterious history of the fazender of Iquitos.

## CHAPTER II.

### THE FIRST MOMENTS.

SCARCELY had the pirogue which bore off Joam Garral, or rather Joam Dacosta—for it is more convenient that he should resume his real name—disappeared, than Benito stepped up to Manoel.

"What is it you know?" he asked.

"I know that your father is innocent! Yes, innocent!" replied Manoel, "and that he was sentenced to death three-and-twenty years ago for a crime which he never committed!"

"He has told you all about it, Manoel?"

"All about it," replied the young man. "The noble fazender did not wish that any part of his past life should be hidden from him who, when he marries his daughter, is to be his second son."

"And the proof of his innocence my father can one day produce?"

"That proof, Benito, lies wholly in the three-and-twenty years of an honorable and honored life, lies entirely in the bearing of Joam Dacosta, who comes forward to say to justice, 'Here am I! I do not care for this false existence any more. I do not care to hide under a name which is not my true one! You have condemned an innocent man! Confess your error and set matters right.'"

"And when my father spoke like that, you did not hesitate for a moment to believe him?"

"Not for an instant," replied Manoel.

The hands of the two young fellows closed in a long and cordial grasp.

Then Benito went up to Padre Passanha.

"Padre," he said, "take my mother and sister away

to their rooms. Do not leave them all day. No one
here doubts my father's innocence—not one, you know
that! To-morrow my mother and I will seek out the
chief of the police. They will not refuse us permis-
sion to visit the prison. No! that would be too cruel.
We will see my father again, and decide what steps
shall be taken to procure his vindication."

Yaquita was almost helpless, but the brave woman,
though nearly crushed by the sudden blow, arose.
With Yaquita Dacosta it was as with Yaquita Garral.
She had not a doubt as to the innocence of her husband. The idea even never occurred to her that Joam
Dacosta had been to blame in marrying her under a
name which was not his own. She only thought of
the life of happiness she had led with the noble man
who had been injured so unjustly. Yes! On the
morrow she would go to the gate of the prison, and
never leave it until it was opened!

Padre Passanha took her and her daughter, who
could not restrain her tears, and the three entered the
house.

The two young fellows found themselves alone.

"And now," said Benito, "I ought to know all that
my father has told you."

"I have nothing to hide from you."

"Why did Torres come on board the jangada?"

"To sell to Joam Dacosta the secret of his past
life."

"And so, when we first met Torres in the forest of
Iquitos, his plan had already been formed to enter into communication with my father?"

"There cannot be a doubt of it," replied Manoel.
"The scoundrel was on his way to the fazenda with
the idea of consummating a vile scheme of extortion
which he had been preparing for a long time."

"And when he learnt from us that my father and
his whole family were about to pass the frontier, he
suddenly changed his line of conduct?"

"Yes. Because Joam Dacosta once in Brazilian
territory became more at his mercy than while within
the frontiers of Peru. That is why we found Torres

at Tabatinga, where he was waiting in expectation of our arrival"

"And it was I who offered him a passage on the raft!" exclaimed Benito, with a gesture of despair.

"Brother," said Manoel, "you need not reproach yourself Torres would have joined us sooner or later. He was not the man to abandon such a trail. Had we lost him at Tabatinga, we should have found him at Manaos."

"Yes, Manoel, you are right. But we are not concerned with the past now. We must think of the present. An end to useless recriminations! Let us see!" And while speaking, Benito, passing his hand across his forehead, endeavored to grasp the details of this strange affair.

"How," he asked, "did Torres ascertain that my father had been sentenced three-and-twenty years back for this abominable crime at Tijuco?"

"I do not know," answered Manoel, "and everything leads me to think that your father did not know that."

"But Torres knew that Garral was the name under which Joam Dacosta was living?"

"Evidently."

"And he knew that it was in Peru, at Iquito, that for so many years my father had taken refuge?"

"He knew it," said Manoel, "but how he came to know it I do not understand."

"One more question," continued Benito. "What was the proposition that Torres made to my father during the short interview which preceded his expulsion?"

"He threatened to denounce Joam Garral as being Joam Dacosta, if he declined to purchase his silence."

"And at what price?"

"At the price of his daughter's hand!" answered Manoel, unhesitatingly, but pale with anger.

"This scoundrel dared to do that!" exclaimed Benito.

"To this infamous request, Benito, you saw the reply that your father gave."

"Yes, Manoel, yes! The indignant reply of an honest man. He kicked Torres off the raft. But it is not enough to have kicked him out. No! That will not do for me. It was on Torres' information that they came here and arrested my father; is not that so?"

"Yes, on his denunciation."

"Very well," continued Benito, shaking his fist toward the left bank of the river, "I must find out Torres. I must know how he became master of the secret. He must tell me if he knows the real author of this crime. He shall speak out. And if he does not speak out, I know what I shall have to do."

"What you will have to do is for me to do as well!" added Manoel, more coolly, but not less resolutely.

"No, Manoel, no, to me alone!"

"We are brothers, Benito," replied Manoel. "The right of demanding an explanation belongs to us both."

Benito made no reply. Evidently on that subject his decision was irrevocable.

At this moment the pilot Araujo, who had been observing the state of the river, came up to them.

"Have you decided," he asked, "if the raft is to remain at her moorings at the Isle of Muras, or to go on to the port of Manaos?"

The question had to be decided before nightfall, and the sooner it was settled the better.

In fact, the news of the arrest of Joam Dacosta ought already to have spread through the town. That it was of a nature to excite the interest of the population of Manaos could scarcely be doubted. But would it provoke more than curiosity against the condemned man, who was the principal author of the crime of Tijuco, which had formerly created such a sensation? Ought they not fear that some popular movement might be directed against the prisoner?

In the face of this hypothesis was it not better to leave the jangada moored near the Isle of Muras on

the right bank of the river at a few miles from Manaos?

"No!" at length exclaimed Benito; "to remain
here would look as though we were abandoning my
father and doubting his innocence—as though we were
afraid to make common cause with him. We must go
to Manaos, and without delay!"

"You are right," replied Manoel. "Let us go!"

Araujo, with an approving nod, began his preparations for leaving the island. The maneuver necessitated a good deal of care. They had to work the raft
slantingly across the current of the Amazon, here
doubled in force by that of the Rio Negro, and to
make for the embouchure of the tributary about a
dozen miles down on the left bank.

The ropes were cast off from the island. The jangada, again started on the river, began to drift off
diagonally. Araujo, cleverly profiting by the bendings
of the current, which were due to the projections of
the banks, and assisted by the long poles of his crew,
succeeded in working the immense raft in the desired
direction.

In two hours the jangada was on the other side of
the Amazon a little above the mouth of the Rio Negro,
and fairly in the current which was to take it to the
lower bank of the vast bay which opened on the left
side of the stream.

At five o'clock in the evening it was strongly moored
alongside this bank, not in the port of Manaos itself,
which it could not enter without stemming a rather
powerful current, but a short mile below it.

The raft was then in the black waters of the Rio
Negro, near rather a high bluff covered with cecropias
with buds of reddish brown, and palisaded with stiff-
stalked reeds called "froxas," of which the Indians
made some of their weapons.

A few citizens were strolling along the bank. A
feeling of curiosity had doubtless attracted them to
the anchorage of the raft. The news of the arrest of
Joam Dacosta had soon spread about, but the curiosi-

ty of the Manaens did not outrun their discretion, and they were very quiet.

Benito's intention had been to land that evening, but Manoel dissuaded him.

"Wait till to-morrow," he said, "night is approaching, and there is no necessity for us to leave the raft."

"So be it! To-morrow," answered Benito.

And here Yaquita, followed by her daughter and Padre Passanha, came out of the house. Minha was still weeping, but her mother's face was tearless, and she had that look of calm resolution which showed that the wife was now ready for all things, either to do her duty or to insist on her rights.

Yaquita slowly advanced towards Manoel.

"Manoel," she said, "listen to what I have to say, for my conscience commands me to speak as I am about to do."

"I am listening," replied Manoel.

Yaquita, looking him straight in the face, continued: "Yesterday, after the interview you had with Joam Dacosta, my husband, you came to me and called me—mother! You took Minha's hand, and called her—your wife! You then knew everything, and the past life of Joam Dacosta had been then disclosed to you."

"Yes," answered Manoel, "and Heaven forbid I should have any hesitation in doing so!"

"Perhaps so," replied Yaquta; "but then Joam Dacosta had not been arrested. The position is not now the same. However innocent he may be, my husband is in the hands of justice; his past life has been publicly proclaimed. Minha is a convict's daughter."

"Minha Dacosta or Mina Garral, what matters it to me?" exclaimed Manoel, who could keep silent no longer.

"Manoel!" murmured Minha.

And she would certainly have fallen, had not Lina's arm supported her.

"Mother, if you do not wish to kill her," said Manoel, "call me your son!"

"My son! my child!"

It was all Yaquita could say, and the tears, which she restrained with difficulty, filled her eyes.

And then they all entered the house. But during the long night not an hour's sleep fell to the lot of the unfortunate family who were so cruelly tried.

---

## CHAPTER III.

### RETROSPECTIVE.

JOAM DACOSTA had relied entirely on Judge Ribeiro, and his death was most unfortunate.

Before he was judge at Manaos, and chief magistrate in the province, Ribeiro had known the young clerk at the time he was being prosecuted for the murder in the diamond arrayal. He was then an advocate at Villa Rica, and he it was who defended the prisoner at the trial. He took the cause to heart and made it his own, and from an examination of the papers and detailed information, and not from the simple fact of his position in the matter, he came to the conclusion that his client was wrongfully accused, and that he had taken not the slightest part in the murder of the escort of the diamonds—in a word, that Joam Dacosta was innocent.

But, notwithstanding this conviction, notwithstanding his talent and zeal, Ribeiro was unable to persuade the jury to take the same view of the matter. How could he remove so strong a presumption? If it was not Joam Dacosta, who had every facility for informing the scoundrels of the convoy's departure, who was it? The official who accompanied the escort had perished with the greater part of the soldiers, and suspicion could not point against him. Everything agreed in distinguishing Dacosta as the true and only author of the crime.

Ribeiro defended him with great warmth and with all his powers, but he could not succeed in saving him. The verdict of the jury was affirmative on all the questions. Joam Dacosta, convicted of aggravated and premeditated murder, did not even obtain the benefit of extenuating circumstances, and heard himself condemned to death.

There was no hope left for the accused. No commutation of the sentence was possible, for the crime was committed in the diamond arrayal. The condemned man was lost. But during the night which preceded his execution, and when the gallows was already erected, Joam Dacosta managed to escape from the prison at Villa Rica. We know the rest.

Twenty years later Ribeiro the advocate became the chief justice of Manaos. In the depths of his retreat the fazender of Iquitos heard of the change, and in it saw a favorable opportunity for bringing forward the revision of the former proceedings against him, with some chance of success. He knew that the old convictions of the advocate wonld be still unshaken in the mind of the judge. He therefore resolved to try and rehabilitate himself. Had it not been for Ribeiro's nomination to the chief justiceship in the province of Amazones, he might perhaps have hesitated, for he had no new material proof of his innocence to bring forward. Although the honest man suffered acutely, he might still have remained hidden in exile at Iquitos, and still have asked for time to smother the remembrances of the horrible occurrence, but something was urging him to act in the matter without delay.

In fact, before Yaquita had spoken to him, Joam Dacosta had noticed that Manoel was in love with his daughter.

The union of the young army doctor and his daughter was in every respect a suitable one. It was evident to Joam that some day or other he would be asked for her hand in marriage, and he did not wish to be obliged to refuse.

But then the thought that his daughter would have to marry under a name which did not belong to her, that Manoel Valdez, thinking he was entering the family of Garral, would enter that of Dacosta, the head of which was under sentence of death. was intolerable to him. No! The wedding should not take place unless under proper conditions! Never!

Let us recall what had happened up to this time. Four years after the young clerk who eventually became the partner of Magalhaes, had arrived at Iquitos, the old Portuguese had been taken back to the farm mortally injured. A few days only were left for him to live. He was alarmed at the thought that his daughter would be left alone and unprotected; but knowing that Joam and Yaquita were in love with each other, he desired their union without delay.

Joam at first refused. He offered to remain the protector or the servant of Yaquita without becoming her husband. The wish of the dying Magalhaes was so urgent that resistance became impossible. Yaquita put her hand into the hand of Joam, and Joam did not withdraw it.

Yes! It was a serious matter! Joam Dacosta ought to have confessed all, or to have fled forever from the house in which he had been so hospitably received, from the establishment of which he had built up the prosperity! Yes! To confess everything rather than to give to the daughter of his benefactor a name which was not his, instead of the name of a felon condemned to death for murder, innocent though he might be!

But the case was pressing, the old fazender was on the point of death, his hands were stretched out towards the young people! Joam was silent, the marriage took place, and the remainder of his life was devoted to the happiness of the girl he had made his wife.

"The day when I confess everything," Joam repeated, "Yaquita will pardon everything! She will not doubt me for an instant! But if I ought not to have deceived her, I certainly will not deceive the honest fellow who wishes to enter our family by marrying Minha! No! I would rather give myself up and have done with this life!"

Many times had Joam thought of telling his wife about his past life. Yes! the avowal was on his lips whenever she asked him to take her into Brazil, and with her and her daughter descend the beautiful Amazon river. He knew sufficient of Yaquita to be sure that her affection for him would not thereby be diminished in the least. But courage failed him !

And this is easily intelligible in the face of the happiness of the family which increased on every side. This happiness was his work, and it might be destroyed for ever by his return.

Such had been his life for those long years ; such had been the continuous source of his sufferings, of which he had kept the secret so well ; such had been the existence of this man, who had no action to be ashamed of, and whom a great injustice compelled to hide away from himself !

But at length the day arrived when there could no longer remain a doubt as to the affection which Manoel bore to Minha, when he could see that a year would not go by before he was asked to give his consent to her marriage, and after a short delay he no longer hesitated to proceed in the matter.

A letter from him, addressed to Judge Ribeiro, acquainted the chief justice with the secret of the existence of Joam Dacosta, with the name under which he was concealed, with the place where he lived with his family, and at the same time with his formal intention of delivering himself up to justice, and taking steps to procure the revision of the proceedings, which would either result in his rehabilitation or in the execution of the iniquitous judgment delivered at Villa Rica.

What were the feelings which agitated the heart of the worthy magistrate? We can easily divine them. It was no longer to the advocate that the accused applied, it was to the chief justice of the province that the convict appealed. Joam Dacosta gave himself over to him entirely, and did not even ask him to keep the secret.

Judge Ribeiro was at first troubled about this unexpected revelation, but he soon recovered himself, and scrupulously considered the duties which the position imposed on him. It was his place to pursue criminals, and here was one who delivered himself into his hands. This criminal, it was true, he had defended; he had never doubted but that he had been unjustly condemned; his joy had been extreme when he saw him escape by flight from the last penalty; he had even instigated and facilitated his flight! But what the advocate had done in the past could the magistrate do in the present?

"Well, yes!" had the judge said, "my conscience tells me not to abandon that just man. The step he is taking is a fresh proof of his innocence, a moral proof, even if he brings me others, which may be the most convincing of all. No! I will not abandon him!"

From this day forward a secret correspondence took place between the magistrate and Joam Dacosta. Ribeiro at the outset cautioned his client against compromising himself by his imprudence. He had again to work up the matter, again to read over the papers, again to look through the inquiries. He had to find out if any new facts had come to light in the diamond province referring to so serious a case. Had any of the accomplices of the crime, of the smugglers who had attacked the convoy, been arrested since the attempt? Had any confessions or half-confessions been brought forward? Joam Dacosta had done nothing but protest his innocence from the very first. But that was not enough, and Judge Ribeiro was desirous of finding in the case itself the clue to the real culprit.

Joam Dacosta had accordingly been prudent. He had promised to be so. But in all his trials it was an immense consolation for him to find his old advocate, though now a chief justice, so firmly convinced that he was not guilty. Yes! Joam Dacosta, in spite of his condemnation, was a victim, a martyr, an honest man to whom society owed a signal reparation! And when the magistrate knew the past career of the fazender of Iquitos since his sentence, the position of his family, all that life of devotion, of work, employed unceasingly for the happiness of those belonging to him, he was not only more convinced but more affected, and determined to do all he could to procure the rehabilitation of the felon of Tijuco.

For six months a correspondence had passed between these two men.

One day, the case being pressing, Joam Dacosta wrote to Judge Ribeiro:

" In two months I will be with you, in the power of the chief justice of the province! "

" Come, then," replied Ribeiro.

The jangada was then ready to go down the river. Joam Dacosta embarked on it with all his people. During the voyage, to the great astonishment of his wife and son, he landed but rarely, as we know. More often he remained shut up in his room, writing, working, not at his trade accounts, but, without saying anything about it, at a kind of memoir, which he called " The History of my Life," and which was meant to be used in the revision of the legal proceedings.

Eight days before his new arrest, made on account of information given by Torres, which forestalled and perhaps would ruin his prospects, he entrusted to an Indian on the Amazon a letter, in which he warned Judge Ribeiro of his approaching arrival.

The letter was sent and delivered as addressed, and the magistrate only waited for Joam Dacosta to commence on the serious undertaking which he hoped to bring to a successful issue.

During the night before the arrival of the raft at Manaos, Judge Ribeiro was seized with an attack of apoplexy. But the denunciation of Torres, whose scheme of extortion had collapsed in face of the noble anger of his victim, had produced its effect. Joam Dacosta was arrested in the bosom of his family, and his old advocate was no longer in this world to defend him.

Yes! the blow was terrible indeed. His lot was cast, whatever his fate might be; there was no going back for him! And Joam Dacosta rose from beneath the blow which had so unexpectedly struck him! It was not only his own honor which was in question, but the honor of all who belonged to him!

# CHAPTER IV.

## MORAL PROOFS.

THE warrant against Joam Dacosta, alias Joam Garral, had been issued by the assistant of Judge Ribeiro, who filled the position of magistrate in the province of Amazones, until the nomination of the successor of the late justice.

This assistant bore the name of Vicente Jarriquez. He was a surly little fellow, whom forty years' practice in criminal procedure had not rendered particularly friendly towards those who came before him. He had had so many cases of this sort, and tried and sentenced so many rascals, that a prisoner's innocence seemed to him *a priori* inadmissable. To be sure, he did not come to a decision unconscientiously; but his conscience was strongly fortified, and was not easily affected by the circumstances of the examination or the arguments for the defense. Like a good many judges, he thought but little of the indulgence of the jury, and when a prisoner was brought before him, after having passed through the sieve of inquest, inquiry, and examination, there was every presumption in his eyes that the man was quite ten times guilty.

Jarriquez, however, was not a bad man. Nervous, fidgety, talkative, keen, crafty, he had a curious look about him, with his big head on his little body; his ruffled hair, which would not have disgraced the judge's wig of the past; his piercing, gimlet-like eyes, with their expression of surprising acuteness; his prominent nose, with which he would assuredly have gesticulated had it been movable; his ears wide open, so as to better catch all that was said, even when it

was out of range of ordinary auditory apparatus; his
fingers unceasingly tapping the table in front of him,
like those of a pianist practising on the mute; and his
body so long and his legs so short, and his feet per-
petually crossing and recrossing, as he sat in state in
his magistrate's chair.

In private life, Jarriquez, who was a confirmed old
bachelor, never left his law books but for the table,
which he did not despise; for chess, of which he was
a past master; and above all things for Chinese puz-
zles, enigmas, charades, rebuses, anagrams, riddles,
and such things, with which, like more than one Euro-
pean justice—thorough sphinxes by taste as well as
by profession—he principally passed his leisure.

It will be seen that he was an original, and it will
be seen also how much Joam Dacosta had lost by the
death of Judge Ribeiro, inasmuch as his case would
come before this not very agreeable judge.

Moreover, the task of Jarriquez was in a way very
simple.  He had neither to inquire nor to rule; he had
not even to regulate a discussion nor to obtain a verdict, neither to apply the articles of the penal code,
nor to pronounce a sentence.  Unfortunately for the
fazender, such formalities were no longer necessary;
Joam Dacosta had been arrested, convicted, and sentenced three-and-twenty years ago for the crime at
Tijuco; no limitation had yet affected his sentence.
No demand in commutation of the penalty could be
introduced, and no appeal for mercy could be received.
It was only necessary then to establish his identity,
and as soon as the order arrived from Rio Janeiro
justice would have taken its course.

But in the nature of things Joam Dacosta would
protest his innocence; he would say he had been unjustly condemned.  The magistrate's duty, notwithstanding the opinions he held, would be to listen to him.
The question would be, what proofs could the convict
offer to make good his assertions ?  And if he was not
able to produce them when he appeared before his
first judges, was he able to do so now?

Herein consisted all the interest of the examination.

There would have to be admitted the fact of a defaulter, prosperous and safe in a foreign country, leaving his refuge of his own free will to face the justice which his past life should have taught him to dread, and herein would be one of those rare and curious cases which ought to interest even a magistrate hardened with all the surroundings of forensic strife. Was it impudent folly on the part of the doomed man of Tijuco, who was tired of his life, or was it the impulse of a conscience which would at all risks have wrong set right? The problem was a strange one, it must be acknowledged.

On the morrow of Joam Dacosta's arrest, Judge Jarriquez made his way to the prison in God-the-Son Street, where the convict had been placed. The prison was an old missionary convent, situated on the bank of one of the principal inguarapes of the town. To the voluntary prisoners of former times there had succeeded in this building, which was but little adapted for the purpose, the compulsory prisoners of to-day. The room occupied by Joam Dacosta was nothing like one of those sad little cells which form part of our modern penitentiary system; but an old monk's room, with a barred window without shutters, opening on to an uncultivated space, a bench in one corner, and a kind of pallet in the other.

It was from this apartment that Joam Dacosta, on this 25th of August, about eleven o'clock in the morning, was taken and brought into the judge's room, which was the old common hall of the convent.

Judge Jarriquez was there in front of his desk, perched on his high chair, his back turned towards the window, so that his face was in shadow while that of the accused remained in full daylight. His clerk, with the indifference which characterizes these legal folks, had taken his seat at the end of the table, his pen behind his ear, ready to record the questions and answers.

Joam Dacosta was introduced into the room, and at a sign from the judge the guards who had brought him withdrew.

Judge Jarriquez looked at the accused for some time. The latter, leaning slightly forward and maintaining a becoming attitude, neither careless nor humble, waited with dignity for the questions to which he was expected to reply.

"Your name?" said Judge Jarriquez.

"Joam Dacosta."

"Your age?"

"Fifty-two."

"Where do you live?"

"In Peru, at the village of Iquitos."

"Under what name?"

"Under that of Garral, which is that of my mother."

"And why do you bear that name?"

"Because for three-and-twenty years I wished to hide myself from the pursuit of Brazilian justice."

The answers were so exact, and seemed to show that Joam Dacosta had made up his mind to confess everything concerning his past life, that Judge Jarriquez, little accustomed to such a course, cocked up his nose more than was usual to him.

"And why," he continued, "should Brazilian justice pursue you?"

"Because I was sentenced to death in 1826 in the diamond affair at Tijuco."

"You confess then that you are Joam Dacosta?"

"I am Joam Dacosta."

All this was said with great calmness, and as simply as possible. The little eyes of Judge Jarriquez, hidden by their lids, seemed to say:

"Never came across anything like this before."

He had put the invariable question which had hitherto brought the invariable reply from culprits of every category protesting their innocence. The fingers of the judge began to beat a gentle tattoo on the table.

"Joam Dacosta," he asked, "what were you doing at Iquitos?"

"I was a fazender, and engaged in managing a farming establishment of considerable size."

"It was prospering?"

"Greatly prospering."

"How long ago did you leave your fazenda?"

"About nine weeks."

"Why?"

"As to that, sir," answered Dacosta, "I invented a pretext, but in reality I had a motive."

"What was the pretext?"

"The responsibility of taking into Para a large raft, and a cargo of different products of the Amazon."

"Ah! and what was the real motive of your departure?"

And in asking this question Jarriquez said to himself:

"Now we shall get into denials and falsehoods."

"The real motive," replied Joam Dacosta, in a firm voice, "was the resolution I had taken to give myself up to the justice of my country."

"You give yourself up!" exclaimed the judge, rising from his stool. "You give yourself up of your own free will?"

"Of my own free will."

"And why?"

"Because I had had enough of this lying life, this obligation to live under a false name, of this impossibility to be able to restore to my wife and children that which belongs to them; in short, sir, because——"

"Because?"

"I was innocent!"

"That is what I was waiting for!" said Judge Jarriquez aside.

And while his fingers tattooed a slightly more audible march, he made a sign with his head to Dacosta, which signified as clearly as possible: "Go on! Tell me your history! I know it, but I do not wish to interrupt you in telling it in your own way."

Joam Dacosta, who did not disregard the magistrate's far from encouraging attitude, could not but see this, and he told the history of his whole life. He spoke quietly without departing from the calm he had imposed upon himself, without omitting any circumstances which had preceded or succeeded his con-

demnation. In the same tone he insisted on the
honored and honorable life he had led since his escape,
and his duties as head of his family, as husband and
father, which he had so worthily fulfilled. He laid
stress only on one circumstance—that which had
brought him to Manaos to urge on the revision of the
proceedings against him, to procure his rehabilitation
—and that he was compelled to do.

Judge Jarriquez, who was naturally prepossessed
against all criminals, did not interrupt him. He contented himself with opening and shutting his eyes like
a man who heard the story told for the hundreth time;
and when Joam Dacosta laid on the table the memoir
which he had drawn up, he made no movement to take
it.

"You have finished?" he said.

"Yes, sir."

"And you persist in asserting that you only left
Iquitos to procure the revision of the judgment against
you?"

"I had no other intention."

"What is there to prove that? Who can prove, that
without the denunciation which brought about your
arrest, you would have given yourself up?"

" This memoir in the first place."

"That memoir was in your possession, and there is
nothing to show that had you not been arrested you
would have put it to the use you say you intended."

"At the least, sir, there was one thing that was not
in my possession, and of the authenticity of which
there can be no doubt."

"What?"

"The letter I wrote to your predecessor, Judge Ribeiro, the letter which gave him notice of my early
arrival."

"Ah! you wrote?"

"Yes. And the letter which ought to have arrived
at its destination should have been handed over to
you."

"Really!" answered Judge Jarriquez, in a slightly
incredulous tone. "You wrote to Judge Ribeiro."

"Before he was a judge in this province," answered Joam Dacosta, "he was an advocate at Villa Rica. He it was who defended me in the trial at Tijuco. He never doubted the justice of my cause. He did all he could to save me. Twenty years later, when he had become chief justice at Manaos, I let him know who I was, where I was, and what I wished to attempt. His opinion about me had not changed, and it was at his advice I left the fazenda, and came in person to proceed with my rehabilitation. But death unfortunately struck him, and maybe I shall be lost, sir, if in Judge Jarriquez I do not find another Judge Ribeiro."

The magistrate, appealed to so directly, was about to start up in defiance of all the traditions of the judicial bench, but he managed to restrain himself, and was contented with muttering:

"Very strong, indeed; very strong!"

Judge Jarriquez was evidently hard of heart, and proof against all surprise.

At this moment a guard entered the room, and handed a sealed package to the magistrate.

He broke the seal and drew a letter from the envelope. He opened it and read it, not without a certain contraction of the eyebrows, and then said:

"I have no reason for hiding from you, Joam Dacosta, that this is the letter you have been speaking about, addressed by you to Judge Ribeiro and sent on to me. I have, therefore, no reason to doubt what you have said on the subject."

"Not only on that subject," answered Dacosta, "but on the subject of all the circumstances of my life which I have brought to your knowledge, and which are none of them open to question."

"Eh! Joam Dacosta," quickly replied Judge Jarriquez. "You protest your innocence; but all prisoners do as much! After all, you only offer moral presumptions. Have you any material proof?"

"Perhaps I have," answered Joam Dacosta.

At these words, Judge Jarriquez left his chair. This was too much for him, and he had to take two or three circuits of the room to recover himself.

## CHAPTER V.

### MATERIAL PROOFS.

WHEN the magistrate had again taken his place,
like a man who considered he was perfectly master of himself, he leaned back in his chair, and with his
head raised and his eyes looking straight in front, as
though not even noticing the accused, remarked in a
tone of the most perfect indifference: "Go on."

Joam Dacosta reflected for a minute, as if hesitating
to resume the order of his thoughts, and then answered as follows:

"Up to the present, sir, I have only given you moral
presumptions of my innocence grounded on the dignity, propriety, and honesty of the whole of my life. I
should have thought that such proofs were those most
worthy of being brought forward in matters of
justice."

Judge Jarriquez could not restrain a movement
of his shoulders, showing that such was not his opinion.

"Since they are not enough, I proceed with the
material proofs which I shall perhaps be able to produce," continued Dacosta; "I say perhaps, for I do
not yet know what credit to attach to them. And, sir,
I have never spoken of these things to my wife or
children, not wishing to raise a hope which might be
destroyed."

"To the point," answered Jarriquez.

"I have every reason to believe, sir, that my
arrest on the eve of the arrival of the raft at Manaos
is due to information given to the chief of the police?"

"You are not mistaken, Joam Dacosta, but I ought to tell you that the information is anonymous."

"It matters little, for I know that it could only come from a scoundrel called Torres."

"And what right have you to speak in such a way of this—informer?"

"A scoundrel! Yes, sir!" replied Joam, quickly. "This man, whom I received with hospitality, only came to me to propose that I should purchase his silence, to offer me an odious bargain that I shall never regret having refused, whatever may be the consequences of his denunciation!"

"Always this method!" thought Judge Jarriguez; "accusing others to clear himself."

But he none the less listened with extreme attention to Joam's recital of his relations with the adventurer up to the moment when Torres let him know that he knew and could reveal the name of the true author of the crime of Tijuco.

"And what is the name of the guilty man?" asked Jarriquez, shaken in his indifference.

"I do not know," answered Joam Dacosta. "Torres was too cautious to let it out."

"And the culprit is living?"

"He is dead."

The fingers of Judge Jarriquez tattooed more quickly, and he could not avoid exclaiming: "The man who can furnish the proof of a prisoner's innocence is always dead."

"If the real culprit is dead, sir," replied Dacosta, "Torres at least is living, and the proof, written throughout in the handwriting of the author of the crime, he has assured me is in his hands ! He offered to sell it to me !"

"Eh ! Joam Dacosta !" answered Judge Jarriquez, "that would not have been dear at the cost of your whole fortune !"

"If Torres had only asked my fortune, I would have given it to him, and not one of my people would have demurred ! Yes, you are right, sir; a man cannot pay too dearly for the redemption of his honor ! But this scoundrel, knowing that I was at his mercy, required more than my fortune!"

" How so ?"

"My daughter's hand was to be the cost of the bargain! I refused ; he denounced me ; and that is why I am now before you!"

"And if Torres had not informed against you," asked Judge ·Jarriquez—"if Torres had not met with you on your voyage, what would you have done on learning on your arrival of the death of Judge Ribeiro? Would you then have delivered yourself into the hands of justice?"

"Without the slightest hesitation," replied Joam, in a firm voice; "for, I repeat it, I had no other object in leaving Iquitos to come to Manaos."

This was said in such a tone of truthfulness, that Judge Jarriquez experienced a kind of feeling making its way to that corner of the heart where convictions are formed, but he did not give in.

He could scarcely help being astonished. A judge engaged merely in this examination, he knew nothing of what is known by those who have followed this history, and who cannot doubt but that Torres held in his hands the material proof of Joam Dacosta's innocence. They know that the document existed; that it contained this evidence ; and perhaps they may be led to think that Judge Jarriquez was pitilessly incredulous. But they should remember that Judge Jarriquez was not in their position; that he was accustomed to the invariable protestations of the culprits who came before him. The document which Joam Dacosta appealed to was not produced; he did not really know if it actually existed; and to conclude, he had before him a man whose guilt had for him the certainty of a settled thing.

However, he wished, perhaps through curiosity, to drive Joam Dacosta behind his last entrenchments.

"And so," he said, "all your hope now rests on the declaration which has been made to you by Torres."

"Yes, sir, if my whole life does not plead for me."

"Where do you think Torres really is?"

"I think in Manaos."

"And you hope that he will speak—that he will consent to good-naturedly hand over to you the document for which you have declined to pay the price he asked?"

"I hope, so, sir," replied Joam Dacosta; "the situation now is not the same for Torres; he has denounced me, and consequently he cannot retain any hope of resuming his bargaining under the previous conditions. But this document might still be worth a fortune if, supposing I am acquitted or executed, it should ever escape him. Hence his interest is to sell me the document, which cannot thus injure him in any way, and I think he will act according to his interest."

The reasoning of Joam Dacosta was unanswerable, and Judge Jarriquez felt it to be so. He made the only possible objection.

"The interest of Torres is doubtless to sell you the document—if the document exists."

"If it does not exist," answered Joam Dacosta, in a penetrating voice, "in trusting to the justice of men, I must put my trust only in God!"

At these words Judge Jarriquez rose, and, in not quite such an indifferent tone, said, "Joam Dacosta, in examining you here, in allowing you to relate the particulars of your past life and to protest your innocence, I have gone further than my instructions allow me. An information has already been laid in this affair, and you have appeared before the jury at Villa Rica, whose verdict was given unanimously and without even the addition of extenuating circumstances. You have been found guilty of the instigation of, and complicity in, the murder of the soldiers and the robbery of the diamonds at Tijuco, the capital sentence was pronounced on you, and it was only by flight that you escaped execution. But that you came here to deliver yourself over, or not, to the hands of justice three-and-twenty years afterwards, you would never have been retaken. For the last time, you admit that you are Joam Dacosta, the condemned man of the diamond arrayal?"

3

"I am Joam Dacosta!"

"You are ready to sign this declaration?"

"I am ready."

And with a hand without a tremble Joam Dacosta put his name to the foot of the declaration and the report which Judge Jarriquez had made his clerk draw up.

"The report, addressed to the minister of justice, is to be sent off to Rio Janeiro," said the magistrate. "Many days will elapse before we receive orders to carry out your sentence. If then, as you say, Torres possesses the proof of your innocence, do all you can yourself—do all you can through your friends—do everything, so that that proof can be produced in time. Once the order arrives no delay will be possible, and justice must take its course."

Joam Dacosta bowed slightly.

"Shall I be allowed in the meantime to see my wife and children?" he asked.

"After to-day, if you wish," answered Judge Jarriquez; "you are no longer in close confinement, and they can be brought to you as soon as they apply."

The magistrate then rang the bell. The guards entered the room, and took away Joam Dacosta.

Judge Jarriquez watched him as he went out, and shook his head, and muttered:

"Well, well! This is a much stranger affair than I ever thought it would be!"

## CHAPTER VI.

### THE LAST BLOW.

WHILE Joam Dacosta was undergoing this examination, Yaquita, from an inquiry made by Manoel, ascertained that she and her children would be
permitted to see the prisoner that very day about four
o'clock in the afternoon.

Yaquita had not left her room since the evening before. Minha and Lina kept near her, waiting for the
time when she would be admitted to see her husband.

Yaquita Garral or Yaquita Dacosta, he would still
find her the devoted wife and brave companion he had
ever known her to be.

About eleven o'clock in the morning Benito joined
Manoel and Fragoso, who were talking in the bow of
the jangada.

"Manoel," said he, "I have a favor to ask you."

"What is it?"

"And you too, Fragoso."

"I am at your service, Mr. Benito," answered the
barber.

"What is the matter?" asked Manoel, looking at
his friend, whose expression was that of a man who
had come to some unalterable resolution.

"You never doubt my father's innocence? Is that
so?" said Benito.

"Ah!" exclaimed Fragoso, "rather I think it was I
who committed the crime."

"Well, we must now commence on the project I
thought of yesterday."

"To find out Torres?" asked Manoel.

"Yes, and know from him how he found out my
father's retreat. There is something inexplicable

about it. Did he know it before? I cannot understand it, for my father never left Iquitos for more than twenty years, and this scoundrel is hardly thirty! But the day will not close before I know it; or, woe to Torres!"

Benito's resolution admitted of no discussion; and besides, neither Manoel nor Fragoso had the slightest thought of dissuading him.

"I will ask, then," continued Benito, "for both of you to accompany me. We shall start in a minute or two. It will not do to wait till Torres has left Manaos. He has no longer got his silence to sell, and the idea might occur to him. Let us be off!"

And so all three of them landed on the bank of the Rio Negro and started for the town.

Manaos was not so considerable that it could not be searched in a few hours. They had made up their minds to go from house to house, if necessary, to look for Torres, but their better plan seemed to be to apply in the first instance to the keepers of the taverns and lojas, where the adventurer was likely to put up. There could hardly be a doubt that the ex-captain of the woods would not have given his name; he might have personal reasons for avoiding all communication with the police. Nevertheless, unless he had left Manaos it was almost impossible for him to escape the young fellows' search. In any case, there would be no use in applying to the police, for it was very probable —in fact, we know that it actually was so—that the information given to them had been anonymous.

For an hour Benito, Manoel, and Fragoso walked along the principal streets of the town, inquiring of tradesmen in their shops, the tavern-keepers in their cabarets, and even the bystanders, without any one being able to recognize the individual whose description they so accurately gave.

Had Torres left Manaos? Would they have to give up all hope of coming across him?

In vain Manoel tried to calm Benito, whose head seemed on fire. Cost what it might, he must get at Torres!

Chance at last favored them, and it was Fragoso who put them on the right track.

In a tavern in Holy Ghost street, from the description which the people received of the adventurer, they replied that the individual in question had put up at the loja the evening before.

"Did he sleep here?" asked Fragoso.

"Yes," answered the tavern-keeper.

"Is he here now?"

"No. He has gone out."

"But he has settled his bill, as a man would who has gone for good?"

"By no means; he left his room about an hour ago, and he will doubtless come back to supper."

"Do you know what road he took when he went out?"

"We saw him turning towards the Amazon, going through the lower town, and you will probably meet him on that side."

Fragoso did not want any more. A few seconds afterwards he rejoined the young fellows, and said:

"I am on the track."

"He is there!" exclaimed Benito.

"No; he has just gone out, and they have seen him walking across to the bank of the Amazon."

"Come on!" replied Benito.

They had to go back towards the river, and the shortest way was for them to take the left bank of the Rio Negro, down to its mouth.

Benito and his companions soon left the last houses of the town behind, and followed the bank, making a slight detour so as not to be observed from the janga-da.

The plain was at this time deserted. Far away the view extended across the flat, where cultivated fields had replaced the former forests.

Benito did not speak; he could not utter a word. Manoel and Fragoso respected his silence. And so the three of them went along and looked about on all sides as they traversed the space between the bank of the Rio Negro and that of the Amazon. Three-quarters of an hour after leaving Manaos, and still they had seen nothing!

Once or twice Indians working in the fields were met with. Manoel questioned them, and one of them at length told him that a man, such as he described, had just passed in the direction of the angle formed by the two rivers at their confluence.

Without waiting for more, Benito, by an irresistible movement, strode to the front, and his two companions had to hurry on to avoid being left behind.

The left bank of the Amazon was then about a quarter of a mile off. A sort of cliff appeared ahead, hiding a part of the horizon, and bounding the view a few hundred paces in advance.

Benito, hurrying on, soon disappeared behind one of the sandy knolls.

"Quicker! quicker!" said Manoel to Fragoso. "We must not leave him alone for an instant."

And they were dashing along when a shot struck on their ears.

Had Benito caught sight of Torres? What had he seen? Had Benito and Torres already met?

Manoel and Fragoso, fifty paces farther on, after swiftly running round one of the spurs of the bank, saw two men standing face to face to each other.

They were Torres and Benito.

In an instant Manoel and Fragoso had hurried up to them. It might have been supposed that in Benito's state of excitement he would be unable to restrain himself when he found himself once again in the presence of the adventurer. It was not so.

As soon as the young man saw himself face to face with Torres, and was certain that he could not escape, a complete change took place in his manner, his coolness returned, and he became once more master of himself.

The two men looked at one another for a few moments without a word.

Torres first broke silence, and in the impudent tone habitual to him, remarked:

"Ah! How goes it, Mr. Benito Garral?"

"No, Benito Dacosta!" answered the young man.

"Quite so," continued Torres. "Mr. Benito Dacosta, accompanied by Mr. Manoel Valdez and my friend Fragoso!"

At the irritating qualification thus accorded him by the adventurer, Fragoso, who was by no means loth to do him some damage, was about to rush to the attack, when Benito, quite unmoved, held him back.

"What is the matter with you, my lad?" exclaimed Torres, retreating for a few steps. "I think I had better put myself on guard."

And as he spoke he drew from beneath his poncho his manchetta, the weapon, adapted at will for offense or defense, which a Brazilian is never without. And then, slightly stooping, and planted firmly on his feet, he waited for what was to follow.

"I have come to look for you, Torres," said Benito, who had not stirred in the least at this threatening attitude.

"To look for me?" answered the adventurer. "It is not very difficult to find me. And why have you come to look for me?"

"To know from your own lips what you appear to know of the past life of my father."

"Really!"

"Yes. I want to know how you recognized him, why you were prowling about our fazenda in the forest of Iquitos, and why you were waiting for us at Tabatiga?"

"Well! it seems to me nothing could be clearer!" answered Torres, with a grin. "I was waiting to get a passage on the jangada, and I went on board with the intention of making him a very simple proposition —which possibly he was wrong in rejecting."

At these words Manoel could stand it no longer. With pale face and eye of fire he strode up to Torres.

Benito, wishing to exhaust every means of conciliation, thrust himself between them.

"Calm yourself, Manoel!" he said. "I am calm— even I!"

And then continuing:

"Quite so, Torres; I know the reason of your coming on board the raft. Possessed of a secret which was doubtless given to you, you wanted to make it a means of extortion. But that is not what I want to know at present."

"What is it, then?"

"I want to know how you recognized Joam Dacosta in the fazender of Iquitos?"

"How I recognized him?" replied Torres. "That is my business, and I see no reason why I should tell you. The important fact is, that I was not mistaken when I denounced in him the real author of the crime of Tijuco!"

"You say that to me!" exclaimed Benito, who began to lose his self-possession.

"I will tell you nothing," returned Torres; "Joam Dacosta declined my propositions! He refused to admit me into his family! Well! now that his secret is known, now that he is a prisoner, it is I who refuse to enter his family, the family of a thief, of a murderer, of a condemned felon, for whom the gallows now waits!"

"Scoundrel!" exclaimed Benito, who drew his manchetta from his belt and put himself in position.

Manoel and Fragoso, by a similar movement, quickly drew their weapons.

"Three against one!" said Torres.

"No! one against one!" answered Benito.

"Really! I should have thought an assassination would have better suited an assassin's son!"

"Torres!" exclaimed Benito, "defend yourself, or I will kill you like a mad dog!"

"Mad! so be it!" answered Torres, "but I bite, Benito Dacosta, and beware of the wounds!"

And then again grasping his manchetta, he put himself on guard and ready to attack his enemy.

Benito had stepped back a few paces.

"Torres," he said, regaining all his coolness, which for a moment he had lost, "you were the guest of my father, you threatened him, you betrayed him, you denounced him, you accused an innocent man, and with God's help I am going to kill you !"

Torres replied with the most insolent smile imaginable. Perhaps at the moment the scoundrel had an idea of stopping any struggle between Benito and him, and he could have done so. In fact, he had seen that Joam Dacosta had said nothing about the document which formed the material proof of his innocence.

Had he revealed to Benito that he, Torres, possessed this proof, Benito would have been that instant disarmed. But his desire to wait till the very last moment, so as to get the very best price for the document he possessed, the recollection of the young man's insulting words, and the hate which he bore to all that belonged to him, made him forget his own interest.

In addition to being thoroughly accustomed to the manchetta, which he often had had occasion to use, the adventurer was strong, active, and artful, so that against an adversary who was scarcely twenty, who could have neither his strength nor his dexterity, the chances were greatly in his favor.

Manoel by a last effort wished to insist on fighting him instead of Benito.

"No, Manoel," was the cool reply, "it is for me alone to avenge my father, and as everything here ought to be in order, you shall be my second."

"Benito!"

"As for you, Fragoso, you will not refuse if I ask you to act as second for that man ?"

"So be it," answered Fragoso, "though it is not an office of honor! Without the least ceremony," he added, "I would have killed him like a wild beast!"

The place where the duel was about to take place was a level bank about fifty paces long, on the top of a cliff rising perpendicularly some fifty feet above the Amazon. The river slowly flowed at the foot, and bathed the clumps of reeds which bristled round its base.

There was, therefore, none too much room, and the

combatant who was the first to give way would quickly be driven over into the abyss.

The signal was given by Manoel, and Torres and
Benito stepped forward.

Benito had complete command over himself. The
defender of a sacred cause, his coolness was unruffled,
much more so than that of Torres, whose conscience,
insensible and hardened as it was, was bound at the
moment to trouble him.

The two met, and the first blow came from Benito.
Torres parried it. They then jumped back, but almost
at the same instant they rushed together, and with
their left hands seized each other by the shoulders—
never to leave go again.

Torres, who was the strongest, struck a side blow
with his manchetta which Benito could not quite parry.
His left side was touched, and his poncho was red-
dened with his blood. But he quickly replied, and
slightly wounded Torres in the hand.

Several blows were then interchanged, but nothing
decisive was done. The ever silent gaze of Benito
peirced the eyes of Torres like a sword blade thrust
to his very heart. Visibly, the scoundrel began to
quail. He recoiled little by little, pressed back by his
implacable foe, who was more determined on taking
the life of his father's denouncer than in defending
his own. To strike was all that Benito longed for;
to parry was all that the other now attempted to do.

Soon Torres saw himself thrust to the very edge of
the bank, at a spot where, slightly scooped away, it
overhung the river. He perceived the danger; he tried
to retake the offensive and regain the lost ground.
His agitation increased, his looks grew livid. At length
he was obliged to stoop beneath the arm which threatened him.

" Die, then!" exclaimed Benito.

The blow was struck full on the chest, but the point
of the manchetta was stopped by a hard substance
hidden beneath the poncho of the adventurer.

Benito renewed his attack, and Torres, whose return thrust did not touch his adversary, felt himself

lost. He was again obliged to retreat. Then he would have shouted—shouted that the life of Joam Dacosta depended on his own! He had not time!

A second thrust of the manchetta pierced his heart. He fell backwards, and the ground suddenly failing him, he was precipitated down the cliff. As a last effort his hands convulsively clutched at a clump of reeds, but they could not stop him, and he disppeared beneath the waters of the river.

Benito was supported on Manoel's shoulder; Fragoso grasped his hands. He would not even give his companions time to dress his wound, which was very slight.

" To the jangada! " he said, " to the jangada! "

Manoel and Fragoso with deep emotion followed him without speaking a word.

A quarter of an hour afterwards the three reached the bank to which the raft was moored. Benito and Manoel rushed into the room where were Yaquita and Minha, and told them all that had passed.

"My son!" "My brother!"

The words were uttered at the same moment.

" To the prison! " said Benito.

" Yes! Come! come! " replied Yaquita.

Benito, followed by Manoel, hurried along his mother, and half an hour later they arrived before the prison.

Owing to the order previously given by Judge Jarriquez they were immediately admitted, and conducted to the chamber occupied by the prisoner.

The door opened.

Joam Dacosta saw his wife, his son, and Manoel enter the room.

"Ah! Joam, my Joam! " exclaimed Yaquita.

" Yaquita! my wife! my children! " replied the prisoner, who opened his arms and pressed them to his heart.

" My Joam, innocent! "

" Innocent and avenged! " said Benito.

"Avenged? What do you mean? "

" Torres is dead, father; killed by my hand! "

"Dead!—Torres!—Dead!" gasped Joam Dacosta.
"My son! You have ruined me!"

## CHAPTER VII.

### RESOLUTIONS.

A FEW hours later the whole family had returned
to the raft, and were assembled in the large room.
All were there, except the prisoner, on whom the last
blow had just fallen. Benito was quite overwhelmed,
and accused himself of having destroyed his father,
and had it not been for the entreaties of Yaquita, of
his sister, of Padre Passanha, and of Manoel, the distracted youth would in the first moments of despair
have probably made away with himself. But he was
never allowed to get out of sight, he was never left
alone. And besides, how could he nave acted otherwise? Ah! why had not Joam Dacosta told him all
before he left the jangada? Why had he refrained
from speaking, except before a judge, of this material
proof of his innocence? Why, in his interview with
Manoel after the expulsion of Torres, had he been
silent about the document which the adventurer pretended to hold in his hands? But, after all, what
faith ought he to place in what Torres had said?
Could he be certain that such a document was in the
rascal's possession?

Whatever might be the reason, the family now knew
everything, and that from the lips of Joam Dacosta
himself. They knew that Torres had declared that
the proof of the innocence of the convict of Tijuco
actually existed; that the document had been written
by the very hand of the author of the attack; that the
criminal, seized by remorse at the moment of his
death, had entrusted it to his companion, Torres; and
that he, instead of fulfilling the wishes of the dying
man, had made the handing over of the document an

excuse for extortion. But they knew also that Torres had just been killed, and that his body was engulfed in the waters of the Amazon, and that he died without even mentioning the name of the guilty man.

Unless he was saved by a miracle, Joam Dacosta might now be considered as irrevocably lost. The death of Judge Ribeiro on the one hand, the death of Torres on the other, were blows from which he could not recover! It should here be said that public opinion at Manaos, unreasoning as it always is, was all against the prisoner. The unexpected arrest of Joam Dacosta had revived the memory of the terrible crime of Tijuco, which had lain forgotten for three-and-twenty years. The trial of the young clerk at the mines of the diamond arrayal, his capital sentence, his escape a few hours before his intended execution—all were remembered, analyzed, and commented on. An article which had just appeared in the *O Diario d'o Grand Para*, the most widely circulated journal in these parts, after giving a history of the circumstances of the crime, showed itself decidedly hostile to the prisoner. Why should these people believe in Joam Dacosta's innocence, when they were ignorant of all that his friends knew—of what they alone knew?

And so the people of Manaos became excited. A mob of Indians and negroes hurried, in their blind folly, to surround the prison and roar forth tumultuous shouts of death. In this part of the two Americas, where executions under Lynch law are of frequent occurrence, the mob soon surrenders itself to its cruel instincts, and it was feared that on this occasion it would do justice with its own hands.

What a night it was for the passengers from the fazenda! Masters and servants had been affected by the blow! Were not the servants of the fazenda members of one family? Every one of them would watch over the safety of Yaquita and her people! On the bank of the Rio Negro there was a constant coming and going of the natives, evidently excited by the arrest of Joam Dacosta, and who could say to what excesses these half-barbarous men might be led?

The time, however, passed without any demonstration against the jangada.

On the morrow, the 26th of August, as soon as the sun rose, Manoel and Fragoso, who had never left Benito for an instant during this terrible night, attempted to distract his attention. After taking him aside they made him understand that there was no time to be lost—that they must make up their minds to act.

"Benito," said Manoel, "pull yourself together! Be a man again! Be a son again!"

"My father!" exclaimed Benito, "I have killed him!"

"No!" replied Manoel. "With heaven's help it is possible that all may not be lost!"

"Listen to us, Mr. Benito," said Fragoso.

The young man, passing his hands over his eyes, made a violent effort to collect himself.

"Benito," continued Manoel, "Torres never gave a hint to put us on the track of his past life. We therefore cannot tell who was the author of the crime of Tijuco, or under what conditions it was committed. To try in that direction is to lose our time!"

"And time presses!" added Fragoso.

"Besides," said Manoel, "suppose we do find out who this companion of Torres was, he is dead, and he could not testify in any way to the innocence of Joam Dacosta. But it is none the less certain that the proof of this innocence exists, and there is no room to doubt the existence of a document which Torres was anxious to make the subject of a bargain. He told us so himself. The document is a complete avowal written in the handwriting of the culprit, which relates the attack in its smallest detail, and which clears our father! Yes! a hundred times, yes! The document exists!"

"But Torres does not exist!" groaned Benito, "and the document has perished with him!"

"Wait, and don't despair yet!" answered Manoel. "You remember under what circumstances we made the acquaintance of Torres? It was in the depths of the forest of Iquitos. He was in pursuit of a monkey which had stolen a metal case, which it so strangely kept, and the chase had lasted a couple of hours when the monkey fell to our guns. Now, do you think it was for the few pieces of gold contained in the case that Torres was in such a fury to recover it? and do you not remember the extraordinary satisfaction which he displayed when we gave him back the case which he had taken out of the monkey's paw?"

"Yes! yes!" answered Benito. "This case which I held—which I gave back to him! Perhaps it con- tained——"

"It is more than probable! It is certain!" replied Manoel.

"And I beg to add," said Fragoso, "for now the fact recurs to my memory, that during the time you were at Ega I remained on board, at Lina's advice, to keep an eye on Torres, and I saw him—yes, I saw him— reading, and again reading, an old, faded paper, and muttering words which I could not understand!"

"That was the document!" exclaimed Benito, who snatched at the hope—the only one that was left. "But this document; had he not put it in some place of security?"

"No," answered Manoel—"no; it was too precious for Torres to dream of parting with it. He was bound to carry it always about with him, and doubtless in that very case!"

"Wait! wait, Manoel!" exclaimed Benito; "I re- member—yes, I remember. During the struggle, at the first blow I struck Torres in his chest, my man- chetta was stopped by some hard substance under his poncho, like a plate of metal——"

"That was the case!" said Fragoso.

"Yes," replied Manoel; "doubt is impossible! That was the case; it was in his breast-pocket."

"But the corpse of Torres?"

"We will recover it!"

"But the paper! The water will have stained it, perhaps destroyed it, or rendered it undecipherable!"

"Why," answered Manoel, "if the metal case which held it was water-tight?"

"Manoel," replied Benito, who seized on the last

hope, "you are right! The corpse of Torres must be recovered! We will ransack the whole of this part of the river, if necessary, but we will recover it!"

The pilot Araujo was then summoned and informed of what they were going to do.

"Good!" replied he; "I know all the eddies and currents where the Rio Negro and the Amazon join, and we shall succeed in recovering the body. Let us take two pirogues, two ubas, a dozen of our Indians, and make a start."

Padre Passanha was then coming out of Yaquita's room.

Benito went to him, and in a few words told him what they were going to do to get possession of the document. "Say nothing to my mother or my sister," he added; "if this last hope fails it will kill them!"

"Go, my lad, go," replied Passanha, "and may God help you in your search!"

Five minutes afterwards the four boats started from the raft. After descending the Rio Negro they arrived near the bank of the Amazon, at the very place where Torres, mortally wounded, had disappeared beneath the waters of the stream.

# CHAPTER VIII.

## THE FIRST SEARCH.

THE search had to commence at once, and that for two weighty reasons.

The first of these was—and this was a question of life or death—that this proof of Joam Dacosta's innocence must be produced before the arrival of the order from Rio Janeiro. Once the identity of the prisoner was established, it was impossible that such an order could be other than the order for his execution.

The second was that the body of Torres should be got out of the water as quickly as possible so as to regain undamaged the metal case and the paper it ought to contain.

At this juncture Araujo displayed not only zeal and intelligence, but also a perfect knowledge of the state of the river at its confluence with the Rio Negro.

"If Torres," he said to the young men, "had been from the first carried away by the current, we should have to drag the river throughout a large area, for we shall have a good many days to wait for his body to reappear on the surface through the effects of decomposition."

"We cannot do that," replied Manoel. "This very day we ought to succeed."

"If, on the contrary," continued the pilot, "the corpse has got stuck among the reeds and vegetation at the foot of the bank, we shall not be an hour before we find it."

"To work, then!" answered Benito.

There was but one way of working. The boats approached the bank, and the Indians, furnished with

long poles, began to sound every part of the river at
the base of the bluff which had served for the scene
of combat.

The place had been easily recognized. A track of
blood stained the declivity in its chalky part, and ran
perpendicularly down it into the water; and there
many a clot scattered on the reeds indicated the very
spot where the corpse had disappeared.

About fifty feet down stream a point jutted out
from the river-side and kept back the waters in a kind
of eddy, as in a large basin. There was no current
whatever near the shore, and the reeds shot up out of
the river unbent. Every hope then existed that Torres' body had not been carried away by the main
stream. Where the bed of the river showed sufficient slope, it was perhaps possible for the corpse to
have rolled several feet along the ridge, and even
there no effect of the current could be traced.

The ubas and the pirogues, dividing the work
among them, limited the field of their researches to
the extreme edge of the eddy, and from the circum-
ference to the centre the crew's long poles left not a
single point unexplored. But no amount of sounding
discovered the body of the adventurer, neither among
the clumps of reeds nor on the bottom of the river,
whose slope was then carefully examined.

Two hours after the work had begun they had been
led to think that the body, having probably struck
against the declivity, had fallen off obliquely and
rolled beyond the limits of this eddy, where the action
of the current commenced to be felt.

" But that is no reason why we should despair," said
Manoel, " still less why we should give up our search."

" Will it be necessary," exclaimed Benito, " to search
the river throughout its breadth and its length ? "

"Throughout its breadth, perhaps," answered
Araujo, " throughout its length, no, fortunately."

"And why ?" asked Manoel.

" Because the Amazon, about a mile away from its
junction with the Rio Negro, makes a sudden bend,
and at the same time its bed rises, so that there is a

kind of natural barrier, well known to sailors as the
Bar of Frias, which things floating near the surface
are alone able to clear. In short, the currents are
ponded back, and they cannot possibly have any effect
over this depression."

This was fortunate, it must be admitted. But was
Araujo mistaken? The old pilot of the Amazon
could be relied on. For the thirty years that he had
followed his profession the crossing of the Bar of Frias,
where the current was increased in force by its decrease
in depth, had often given him trouble. The narrow-
ness of the channel and the elevation of the bed made
the passage exceedingly difficult, and many a raft had
there come to grief.

And so Araujo was right in declaring that if the
corpse of Torres was still retained by its weight on the
sandy bed of the river, it could not have been dragged
over the bar. It is true that, later on, when, on account
of the expansion of the gases, it would again rise to
the surface, the current would bear it away, and it
would be irrecoverably lost down the stream, a long
way beyond the obstruction. But this purely physical
effect would not take place for several days.

They could not have applied to a man who was more
skilful or more conversant with the locality than
Araujo, and when he affirmed that the body could not
have been borne out of the narrow channel for more
than a mile or so, they were sure to recover it if they
thoroughly sounded that portion of the river.

Not an island, not an inlet, checked the course of
the Amazon in these parts. Hence, when the foot of
the two banks had been visited up to the bar, it was
in the bed itself, about five hundred feet in width,
that more careful investigations had to be commenced.

The way the work was conducted was this: The
boats taking the right and left of the Amazon lay
alongside the banks. The reeds and vegetation were
tried with the poles. Of the smallest ledges in the
banks in which a body conld rest, not one escaped the
scrutiny of Araujo and his Indians.

But all this labor produced no result, and half the day had elapsed without the body being brought to the surface of the stream.

An hour's rest was given to the Indians. During this time they partook of some refreshment, and then they returned to their task.

Four of the boats, in charge of the pilot, Benito, Fragoso, and Manoel, divided the river between the Rio Negro and the Bar of Frias into four portions. They set to work to explore its very bed. In certain places the poles proved insufficient to thoroughly search among the deeps, and hence a few dredges— or rather harrows, made of stones and old iron, bound round with a solid bar—were taken on board, and when the boats had pushed off these rakes were thrown in and the river bottom stirred up in every direction.

It was in this difficult task that Benito and his companions were employed till the evening. The ubas and pirogues, worked by the oars, traversed the whole surface of the river up to the Bar of Frias.

There had been moments of excitement during this spell of work, when the harrows, catching in something at the bottom, offered some slight resistance. They were then hauled up, but in place of the body so eagerly searched for, there would appear only heavy stones or tufts of herbage which they had dragged from their sandy bed. No one, however, had an idea of giving up the enterprise. They none of them thought of themselves in this work of salvation. Benito, Manoel, Araujo had not even to stir up the Indians or to encourage them. The gallant fellows knew that they were working for the fazender of Iquitos—for the man whom they loved, for the chief of the excellent family who treated their servants so well.

Yes; and so they would have passed the night in dragging the river. Of every minute lost all knew the value.

A little before the sun disappeared, Araujo, finding it useless to continue his operations in the gloom, gave the signal for the boats to join company and return together to the confluence of the Rio Negro and regain the jangada.

The work so carefully and intelligently conducted was not, however, at an end.

Manoel and Fragoso, as they came back, dared not mention their ill-success before Benito. They feared that the disappointment would only force him to some act of despair.

But neither courage nor coolness deserted the young fellow; he was determined to follow to the end this supreme effort to save the honor and the life of his father, and he it was who addressed his companions, and said: "To-morrow we will try again, and under better conditions if possible."

"Yes," answered Manoel; "you are right, Benito. We can do better. We cannot pretend to have entirely explored the river along the whole of the banks and over the whole of its bed."

"No; we cannot have done that," replied Araujo; "and I maintain what I said—that the body of Torres is there, and that it is there because it has not been carried away, because it could not be drawn over the Bar of Frias, and because it will take many days before it rises to the surface and floats down the stream. Yes, it is there, and not a demijohn of tafia will pass my lips until I find it!"

This affirmation from the pilot was worth a good deal, and was of a hope-inspiring nature.

However, Benito, who did not care so much for words as he did for things, thought proper to reply: "Yes, Araujo; the body of Torres is in the river, and we shall find it if——"

"If?" said the pilot.

"If it has not become the prey of the alligators!"

Manoel and Fragoso waited anxiously for Araujo's reply.

The pilot was silent for a few moments; they felt that he was reflecting before he spoke. "Mr. Benito," he said, at length, "I am not in the habit of speaking lightly. I had the same idea as you; but listen.

During the ten hours we have been at work have you seen a single cayman in the river?"

"Not one!" said Fragoso.

"If you have not seen one," continued the pilot, "it was because there were none to see, for these animals have nothing to keep them in the white waters when, a quarter of a mile off, there are large stretches of the black waters, which they so greatly prefer. When the raft was attacked by some of these creatures it was in a part where there was no place for them to flee to. Here it is quite different. Go to the Rio Negro, and there you will see caymans by the score. Had Torres' body fallen into that tributary there might be no chance of recovering it. But it was in the Amazon that it was lost, and in the Amazon it will be found!"

Benito, relieved from his fears, took the pilot's hand and shook it, and contented himself with the reply: "To-morrow, my friends!"

Ten minutes later they were all on board the jangada. During the day Yaquita had passed some hours with her husband. But before she started, and when she saw neither the pilot, nor Manoel, nor Benito, nor the boats, she had guessed the search on which they had gone, but she said nothing to Joam Dacosta, as she hoped that in the morning she would be able to inform him of their success.

But when Benito set foot on the raft she perceived that their search had been fruitless. However, she advanced towards him. "Nothing?" she asked.

"Nothing," replied Benito. "But the morrow is left to us."

The members of the family retired to their rooms, and nothing more was said as to what had passed.

Manoel tried to make Benito lie down so as to take a few hours' rest.

"What is the good of that?" asked Benito. "Do you think I could sleep?"

## CHAPTER IX.

### THE SECOND ATTEMPT.

ON the morrow, the 27th of August, Benito took
Manoel apart, before the sun had risen, and said
to him : "Our yesterday's search was vain. If we begin again under the same conditions, we may be just
as unlucky."

"We must do so, however," replied Manoel.

"Yes," continued Benito ; "but suppose we do not
find the body, can you tell me how long it will be before it will rise to the surface ? "

"If Torres," answered Manoel, "had fallen into
the water living, and not mortally wounded, it would
take five or six days ; but if he had only disappeared
after being so wounded, perhaps two or three days
would be enough to bring him up again."

This answer of Manoel, which was quite correct, requires some explanation. Every human body which
falls into the water will float if equilibrium is established between its density and that of its liquid bed.
This is well known to be the fact, even when a person
does not know how to swim. Under such circumstances, if you are entirely submerged, and only keep
your mouth and nose away from the water, you are
sure to float. But this is not generally done. The
first movement of a drowning man is to try and hold
as much as he can of himself above water; he holds
up his head and lifts up his arms, and these parts of
his body, being no longer supported by the liquid, do
not lose that amount of weight which they would do
if completely immersed. Hence an excess of weight,
and eventually entire submersion, for the water makes

its way to the lungs through the mouth, takes the place of the air which fills them, and the body sinks to the bottom.

On the other hand, when the man who falls into the water is already dead, the conditions are different, and more favorable for his floating, for then the movements of which we have spoken are checked, and the liquid does not make its way to the lungs so copiously, as there is no attempt to respire, and he is consequently more likely to promptly reappear. Manoel then was right in drawing the distinction between the man who falls into the water living and the man who falls into it dead. In the one case the return to the surface takes much longer than in the other.

The reappearance of the body after an immersion more or less prolonged, is always determined by the decomposition, which causes the gases to form. These bring about the expansion of the cellular tissues, the volume augments and the weight decreases, and then, weighing less than the water it displaces, the body attains the proper conditions for floating.

"And thus," continued Manoel, "supposing the conditions continue favorable, and Torres did not live after he fell into the water, if the decomposition is not modified by circumstances which we cannot foresee, he will not reappear bfore three days."

"We have not got three days," answered Benito. "We cannot wait, you know; we must try again, and in some new way."

"What can you do?" answered Manoel.

"Plunge down myself beneath the waters," replied Benito, "and search with my eyes—with my hands."

"Plunge in a hundred times—a thousand times!" exclaimed Manoel. "So be it. I think, like you, that we ought to go straight at what we want, and not struggle on with poles and drag like a blind man, who only works by touch. I also think that we cannot wait three days. But to jump in, come up again, and go down again will give only a short period for the exploration. No; it will never do and we shall only risk a second failure."

"Have you no other plan to propose, Manoel?" asked Benito, looking earnestly at his friend.

"Well, listen. There is what would seem to be a Providential circumstance that may be of use to us."

"What is that?"

"Yesterday, as we hurried through Manaos, I noticed that they were repairing one of the quays on the bank of the Rio Negro. The submarine works were being carried on with the aid of a diving-dress. Let us borrow, or hire, or buy, at any price, this apparatus, and then we may resume our researches under more favorable conditions."

"Tell Araujo, Fragoso, and our men, and let us be off," was the instant reply of Benito.

The pilot and the barber were informed of the decision with regard to Manoel's project. Both were ordered to go with the four boats and the Indians to the basin of Frias, and thence to wait for the two young men.

Manoel and Benito started off without losing a moment, and reached the quay at Manaos. There they offered the contractor such a price that he put the apparatus at their service for the whole day.

"Will you not have one of my men," he asked, "to help you?"

"Give us your foreman and one of his mates to work the air-pump," replied Manoel.

"But who is going to wear the diving-dress?"

"I am," answered Benito.

"You !" exclaimed Manoel.

"I intend to do so."

It was useless to resist.

An hour afterwards the raft and all the instruments necessary for the enterprise had drifted down to the bank where the boats were waiting.

The diving-dress is well-known. By its means men can descend beneath the waters and remain there a certain time without the action of the lungs being in any way injured. The diver is clothed in a waterproof suit of india rubber, and his feet are attached to leaden shoes, which allow him to retain his upright

position beneath the surface. At the collar of the
dress, and about the hight of the neck, there is fitted
a collar of copper, on which is screwed a metal globe
with a glass front. In this globe the diver places his
head, which he can move about at ease. To the globe
are attached two pipes ; one used for carrying off the
air ejected from the lungs, and which is unfit for respiration, and the other in communication with a
pump worked on the raft, and bringing in the fresh
air. When the diver is at work the raft remains im-
movable above him ; when the diver moves about on
the bottom of the river the raft follows his movements,
or he follows those of the raft, according to his con-
venience.

These diving-dresses are now much improved, and
are less dangerous than formerly. The man beneath
the liquid mass can easily bear the additional pressure,
and if anything was to be feared below the waters it
was rather some cayman who might there be met with.
But, as had been observed by Araujo, not one of
these amphibians had been seen, and they are well-
known to prefer the black waters of the tributaries of
the Amazon. Besides, in case of danger, the diver has
always his check-string fastened to the raft, and at the
least warning can be quickly hauled to the surface.

Benito, invariably very cool once his resolution was
taken, commenced to put his idea into execution, and
got into the diving-dress. His head disappeared in
the metal globe, his hand grasped a sort of iron spar
with which to stir up the vegetation and detritus accumulated in the river-bed, and on his giving the
signal he was lowered into the stream.

The men on the raft immediately commenced to
work the air pump, while four Indians from the jangada, under the orders of Araujo, gently propelled it
with their long poles in the desired direction.

The two pirogues, commanded one by Fragoso, the
other by Manoel, escorted the raft, and held themselves ready to start in any direction, should Benito
find the corpse of Torres and again bring it to the surface of the Amazon.

## CHAPTER X.

### A CANNON SHOT.

BENITO then had disappeared beneath the vast
sheet which still covered the corpse. of the adventurer. Ah! If he had had the power to divert the
waters of the river, to turn them into vapor, or to
turn them off—if he could have made the Frias basin
dry down stream, from the bar up to the influx of the
Rio Negro, the case hidden in Torres' clothes would
already have been in his hands! His father's innocence would have been recognized! Joam Dacosta,
restored to liberty, would have again started on the
descent of the river, and what terrible trials would
have been avoided!

Benito had reached the bottom. His heavy shoes
made the gravel on the beach crunch beneath them.
He was in some ten or fifteen feet of water, at the
base of the cliff, which was here very steep, and at
the very spot where Torres had disappeared.

Near him was a tangled mass of reeds and twigs
and aquatic plants, all laced together, which assuredly
during the researches of the previous day no pole
could have penetrated. It was consequently possible
that the body was entangled among the submarine
shrubs, and still in the place where it had originally
fallen.

Hereabouts, thanks to the eddy produced by the
prolongation of one of the spurs running out into the
stream, the current was absolutely nil. Benito guided
his movements by those of the raft, which the long
poles of the Indians kept just over his head.

The light penetrated deep through the clear waters,
and the magnificent sun, shining in a cloudless sky,

shot its rays down into them unchecked. Under ordinary conditions, at a depth of some twenty feet in water, the view becomes exceedingly blurred, but here the waters seemed to be impregnated with a luminous fluid, and Benito was able to descend still lower without the darkness concealing the river bed.

The young man slowly made his way along the bank. With his iron-shod spear he probed the plants and rubbish accumulated along its foot. Flocks of fish, if we can use such an expression, escaped on all sides from the dense thickets like flocks of birds. It seemed as though the thousand pieces of a broken mirror glimmered through the waters. At the same time scores of crustaceans scampered over the sand, like huge ants hurrying from their hills.

Notwithstanding that Benito did not leave a single point of the river unexplored, he never caught sight of the object of his search. He noticed, however, that the slope of the river-bed was very abrupt, and he concluded that Torres had rolled beyond the eddy towards the centre of the stream. If so, he would probably still recover the body, for the current could hardly touch it at the depth which was already great, and seemed sensibly to increase. Benito then resolved to pursue his investigations on the side where he had begun to probe the vegetation. This was why he continued to advance in that direction, and the raft had to follow him during a quarter of an hour, as had been previously arranged.

The quarter of an hour had elapsed, and Benito had found nothing. He felt the need of ascending to the surface, so as to once more experience those physiological conditions in which he could recoup his strength. In certain spots, where the depth of the river necessitated it, he had had to descend about thirty feet. He had thus to support a pressure almost equal to an atmosphere, with the result of the physical fatigue and mental agitation which attack those who are not used to this kind of work. Benito then pulled the communication cord, and the men on the raft commenced to haul him in, but they worked slowly, taking a minute to draw him up two or three feet, so as not to produce in his internal organs the dreadful effects of decompression.

As soon as the young man had set foot on the raft, the metallic sphere of the diving dress was raised, and he took a long breath and sat down to rest.

The pirogues immediately rowed alongside. Manoel, Fragoso and Araujo came close to him, waiting for him to speak.

" Well ? " asked Manoel.

" Still nothing ! Nothing ! "

" Have you not seen a trace ? "

" Not one ! "

" Shall I go down now ? "

" No, Manoel," answered Benito ; " I have begun ; I know where to go. Let me do it ! "

Benito then explained to the pilot that his intention was to visit the lower part of the bank up to the bar of Frias, for there the slope had perhaps stopped the corpse, if, floating between the two streams, it had in the least degree been affected by the current. But first he wanted to skirt the bank and carefully explore a sort of hole formed in the slope of the bed, to the bottom of which the poles had not been able to penetrate. Arraujo aproved of the plan, and made the necessary preparations.

Manoel gave Benito a little advice. " As you want to pursue your search on that side," he said, " the raft will have to go over there obliquely; but mind what you are doing, Benito. That is much deeper than where you have been yet: it may be fifty or sixty feet, and you will have to support a pressure of quite two atmospheres. Only venture with extreme caution, or you may lose your presence of mind, and no longer know where you are or what to do. If your head feels as if in a vise, and your ears tingle, do not hesitate to give us the signal, and we will at once haul you up. You can then begin again if you like, as you will have got accustomed to move about in the deeper parts of the river."

Benito promised to attend to these hints, of which

he recognized the importance. He was particularly struck with the fact that his presence of mind might abandon him at the very moment he wanted it most.

Benito shook hands with Manoel; the sphere of the diving-dress was again screwed to his neck, the pump began to work, and the diver once more disappeared beneath the stream.

The raft was then taken about forty feet along the left bank, but as it moved toward the center of the river the current increased in strength, the ubas was moored, and the rowers kept it from drifting, so as only to allow it to advance with extreme slowness.

Benito descended very gently, and again found himself on the firm sand. When his heels touched the ground it could be seen, by the length of the haulage cord, that he was at a depth of some sixty-five or seventy feet. He was therefore in a considerable hole, excavated far below the ordinary level.

The liquid medium was more obscure, but the limpidity of these transparent waters still allowed the light to penetrate sufficiently for Benito to distinguish the objects scattered on the bed of the river, and to approach them with some safety. Besides, the sand, sprinkled with mica flakes, seemed to form a sort of reflector, and the very grains could be counted glittering like luminous dust.

Benito moved on, examining and sounding the smallest cavities with his spear. He continued to advance very slowly ; the communication cord was paid out, and as the pipes which served for the inlet and outlet of the air were never tightened, the pump was worked under the proper conditions.

Benito turned off so as to reach the middle of the bed of the Amazon, where there was the greatest depression. Sometimes profound obscurity thickened around him, and then he could see nothing, so feeble was the light ; but this was a purely passing phenomenon, and due to the raft, which, floating above his head, intercepted the solar rays, and made the night replace the day. An instant afterwards the huge shadow would be dissipated, and the reflection of the sands appear again in full force.

All the time Benito was going deeper. He felt the increase of the pressure with which his body was wrapped by the liquid mass. His respiration became less easy ; the retractibility of his organs no longer worked with as much ease as in the midst of an atmosphere more conveniently adapted for them. And so he found himself under the action of physiological effects to which he was unaccustomed. The rumbling grew louder in his ears, but as his thought was always lucid, as he felt that the action of his brain was quite clear—even a little more so than usual—he delayed giving the signal for return, and continued to go down deeper still.

Suddenly, in the subdued light which surrounded him, his attention was attracted by a confused mass. It seemed to take the form of a corpse, entangled beneath a clump of aquatic plants. Intense excitement seized him. He stepped towards the mass ; with his spear he felt it. It was the carcass of a huge cayman, already reduced to a skeleton, and which the current of the Rio Negro had swept into the bed of the Amazon. Benito recoiled, and, in spite of the assertions of the pilot, the thought recurred to him that some living cayman might even then be met with in the deeps near the bar of Frias !

But he repelled the idea, and continued his progress, so as to reach the very bottom of the depression.

And now he had arrived at a depth of from eighty to a hundred feet, and consequently was experiencing a pressure of three atmospheres. If, then, this cavity was also drawn blank, he would have to suspend his researches.

Experience has shown that the extreme limit for such submarine explorations lies between a hundred and twenty and a hundred and thirty feet, and that below this there is great danger, the human organism not only being hindered from performing its functions under such a pressure, but the apparatus failing to keep up a sufficient supply of air with the desirable regularity.

But Benito was resolved to go as far as his mental powers and physical energies would let him. By some strange presentiment he was drawn towards this abyss; it seemed to him as though the corpse was very likely to have rolled to the bottom of the hole, and that Torres, if he had any heavy things about him, such as a belt containing either money or arms, would have sunk to the very lowest point. Of a sudden, in a deep hollow, he saw a body through the gloom! Yes! A corpse, still clothed, stretched out like a man asleep, with his arms folded under his head.

Was that Torres? In the obscurity, then very dense, he found it difficult to see; but it was a human body that lay there, less than ten paces off, and perfectly motionless.

A sharp pang shot through Benito. His heart, for an instant, ceased to beat. He thought he was going to lose consciousness. By a supreme effort he recovered himself. He stepped towards the corpse.

Suddenly a shock as violent as unexpected made his whole frame vibrate! A long whip seemed to twine round his body, and in spite of the thick diving-dress he felt himself lashed again and again.

"A gymnotus!" he said.

It was the only word that passed his lips.

In fact, it was a "puraque," the name given by the Brazilians to the gymnotus, or electric snake, which had just attacked him.

It is well known that the gymnotus is a kind of eel, with a blackish, slimy skin, furnished along the back and tail with an apparatus composed of plates joined by vertical lamellæ, and acted on by nerves of considerable power. This apparatus is endowed with singular electrical properties, and is apt to produce very formidable results. Some of these gymnotuses are about the length of a common snake, others are about ten feet long, while others, which, however, are rare, even reach fifteen or twenty feet, and are from eight to ten inches in diameter.

Gymnotuses are plentiful enough both in the Amazon and its tributaries ; and it was one of these living coils, about ten feet long, which, after uncurving itself like a bow, again attacked the diver.

Benito knew what he had to fear from this formidable animal. His clothes were powerless to protect him. The discharges of the gymnotus, at first somewhat weak, became more and more violent, and there would come a time when, exhausted by the shocks, he would be rendered powerless.

Benito, unable to resist the blows, half dropped upon the sand. His limbs were becoming paralyzed little by little under the electric influences of the gymnotus, which lightly touched his body as it wrapped him in its folds. His arms even he could not lift, and soon his spear escaped him, and his hand had not strength enough left to pull the cord and give the signal.

Benito felt that he was lost. Neither Manoel nor his companions could suspect the horrible combat which was going on beneath them between the formidable puraque and the unhappy diver, who only fought to suffer, without any power of defending himself.

And that at the moment when a body—the body of Torres without a doubt !—had just met his view.

By a supreme instinct of self-preservation Benito uttered a cry. His voice was lost in the metallic sphere from which not a sound could escape !

And now the puraque redoubled its attacks ; it gave forth shock after shock, which made Benito writhe on the sand like the sections of a divided worm, and his muscles were wrenched again and again beneath the living lash!

Benito thought that all was over; his eyes grew dim, his limbs began to stiffen.

But before he quite lost his power of sight and reason he became the witness of a phenomenon, unexpected, inexplicable, and marvellous in the extreme.

A deadened roar resounded through the liquid depths. It was like a thunder-clap, the reverberations of which rolled along the river bed, then violently agitated by the electrical discharges of the gymnotus. Benito felt himself bathed as it were in the dreadful booming which found an echo in the very deepest of the river deeps.

And then a last cry escaped him, for fearful was the vision which appeared before his eyes!

The corpse of the drowned man which had been stretched on the sand arose! The undulations of the water lifted up the arms, and they swayed about as if with some peculiar animation. Convulsive throbs made the movement of the corpse still more alarming.

It was indeed the body of Torres. One of the sun's rays shot down to it through the liquid mass, and Benito recognized the bloated, ashy features of the scoundrel who fell by his own hand, and whose last breath had left him beneath the waters.

And while Benito could not make a single movement with his paralyzed limbs, while his heavy shoes kept him down as if he had been nailed to the sand, the corpse straightened itself up, the head swayed to and fro, and disentangling itself from the hole in which it had been kept by a mass of aquatic weeds, it slowly ascended to the surface of the Amazon.

## CHAPTER XI.

### THE CONTENTS OF THE CASE.

WHAT was it that had happened ?   A purely physical phenomenon, of which the following is an
explanation.

The gunboat " Santa Ana," bound for Manaos, had
come up the river and passed the bar at Frias.   Just
before she reached the embouchure of the Rio Negro
she hoisted her colors and saluted the Brazilian flag.

At the report vibrations were produced along the
surface of the stream, and these vibrations making
their way down to the bottom of the river, had been
sufficient to raise the corpse of Torres, already light-
ened by the commencement of its decomposition and
the distention of its cellular system.   The body of the
drowned man had in the ordinary course risen to the
surface of the water.

This well-known phenomenon explains the reappearance of the corpse, but it must be admitted that the
arrival of the " Santa Ana " was a fortunate coinci-
dence.

By a shout from Manoel, repeated by all his companions, one of the pirogues was immediately steered
for the body while the diver was at the same time
hauled up to the raft.

Great was Manoel's emotion when Benito, drawn on
to the platform, was laid there in a state of complete
inertia, not a single exterior movement betraying
that he still lived.

Was not this a second corpse which the waters of
the Amazon had given up ?

As quickly as possible the diving-dress was taken
off him.

Benito had entirely lost consciousness beneath the violent shocks of the gymnotus.

Manoel, distracted, called to him, breathed into him, and endeavored to recover the heart's pulsation.

"It beats!   It beats!" he exclaimed.

Yes!   Benito's heart did still beat, and in a few minutes Manoel's efforts restored him to life.

"The body! the body!"

Such were the first words, the only ones which escaped from Benito's lips.

"There it is!" answered Fragoso, pointing to a pirogue then coming up to the raft with the corpse.

"But what has been the matter, Benito?" asked Manoel.   "Has it been the want of air?"

"No!" said Benito; "a puraque attacked me! But the noise? the detonation?"

"A cannon shot!" replied Manoel.   "It was the cannon shot which brought the corpse to the surface."

At this moment the pirogue came up to the raft with the body of Torres, which had been taken on board by the Indians.   His sojourn in the water had not disfigured him very much.   He was easily recognizable, and there was no doubt as to his identity.

Fragoso, kneeling down in the pirogue, had already begun to undo the clothes of the drowned man, which came away in fragments.

At the moment, Torres' right arm, which was now left bare, attracted his attention.   On it appeared the distinct scar of an old wound produced by a blow from a knife.

"That scar!" exclaimed Fragoso.   "But—that is good! I remember now——"

"What?" demanded Manoel.

"A quarrel!   Yes! a quarrel I witnessed in the province of Madeira three years ago.   How could I have forgotten it!   This Torres was then a captain of the woods.   Ah!   I know now where I had seen him, the scoundrel!"

"That does not matter to us now!" cried Benito.

"The case! the case!   Has he still got that?" and

Benito was about to tear away the last coverings of the corpse to get at it.

Manoel stopped him.

"One moment, Benito," he said; and then, turning to the men on the raft who did not belong to the jangada, and whose evidence could not be suspected at any future time—

"Just take note, my friends," he said, "of what we are doing here, so that you can relate before the magistrate what has passed."

The men came up to the pirogue.

Fragoso undid the belt which encircled the body of Torres underneath the torn poncho, and feeling his breastpocket, exclaimed:

"The case!"

A cry of joy escaped from Benito. He stretched forward to seize the case, to make sure that it contained——

"No!" again interrupted Manoel, whose coolness did not forsake him. "It is necessary that not the slightest possible doubt should exist in the mind of the magistrate! It is better that disinterested witnesses should affirm that this case was really found on the corpse of Torres!"

"You are right," replied Benito.

"My friend," said Manoel to the foreman of the raft, "just feel in the pocket of the waistcoat."

The foreman obeyed. He drew forth a metal case, with the cover screwed on, and which seemed to have suffered in no way from its sojourn in the water.

"The paper! Is the paper still inside?" exclaimed Benito, who could not contain himself.

"It is for the magistrate to open this case!" answered Manoel. "To him belongs the duty of verifying that the document was found within it."

"Yes, yes. Again you are right, Manoel," said Benito. "To Manaos, my friends—to Manaos!"

Benito, Manoel, Fragoso, and the foreman, who held the case, immediately jumped into one of the pirogues, and were starting off, when Fragoso said:

"And the corpse?"

The pirogue stopped.

In fact, the Indians had already thrown back the body into the water, and it was drifting away down the river.

"Torres was only a scoundrel," said Benito. "If I had to fight him, it was God that struck him, and his body ought not to go unburied!"

And so orders were given to the second pirogue to recover the corpse, and take it to the bank to await its burial.

But at the same moment a flock of birds of prey, which skimmed along the surface of the stream, pounced on the floating body. They were urubus, a kind of small vulture, with naked necks and long claws, and black as crows. In South America they are known as gallinazos, and their voracity is unparalleled. The body, torn open by their beaks, gave forth the gases which inflated it, its density increased, it sank down little by little, and for the last time what remained of Torres disappeared beneath the waters of the Amazon.

Ten minutes afterwards the pirogue arrived at Manaos. Benito and his companions jumped ashore, and hurried through the streets of the town. In a few minutes they had reached the dwelling of Judge Jarriquez, and informed him, through one of his servants, that they wished to see him immediately.

The judge ordered them to be shown into his study.

There Manoel recounted all that had passed, from the moment when Torres had been killed until the moment when the case had been found on his corpse, and taken from his breast-pocket by the foreman.

Although this recital was of a nature to corroborate all that Joam Dacosta had said on the subject of Torres, and of the bargain which he had endeavored to make, Judge Jarriquez could not restrain a smile of incredulity.

"There is the case, sir," said Manoel. "For not a single instant has it been in our hands, and the man who gives it to you is he who took it from the body of Torres."

The magistrate took the case and examined it with care, turning it over and over as though it were made of some precious material. Then he shook it, and a few coins inside sounded with a metallic ring. Did not, then, the case contain the document which had been so much sought after—the document written in the very hand of the true author of the crime of Ti-juco, and which Torres had wished to sell at such an ignoble price to Joam Dacosta? Was this material proof of the convict's innocence irrecoverably lost?

We can easily imagine the violent agitation which had seized upon the spectators of this scene. Benito could scarcely utter a word; he felt his heart ready to burst. "Open it, sir! open the case!" he at last exclaimed, in a broken voice.

Judge Jarriquez began to unscrew the lid; then, when the cover was removed, he turned up the case, and from it a few pieces of gold dropped out and rolled on the table.

"But the paper! the paper!" again gasped Benito, who clutched hold of the table to save himself from falling.

The magistrate put his fingers into the case and drew out, not without difficulty, a faded paper, folded with care, and which the water did not seem to have touched.

"The document! that is the document!" shouted Fragoso; "that is the very paper I saw in the hands of Torres!"

Judge Jarriquez unfolded the paper and cast his eyes over it, and then he turned it over so as to examine it on the back and the front, which were both covered with writing. "A document it really is!" said he; "there is no doubt of that. It is indeed a document!"

"Yes," replied Benito; "and that is the document which proves my father's innocence!"

"I do not know that," replied Judge Jarriquez; "and I am afraid it will be very difficult to know it."

"Why?" exclaimed Benito, who became pale as death.

"Because this document is a cryptogram, and ——
"Well?"
"We have not got the key!"

———

## CHAPTER XII.

### THE DOCUMENT.

THIS was a contingency which neither Joam Dacosta nor his people could have anticipated. In fact, as those who have not forgotten the first scene in this story are aware, the document was written in a disguised form in one of the numerous systems used in cryptography.

But which of them?

To discover this would require all the ingenuity of which the human brain was capable.

Before dismissing Benito and his companions, Judge Jarriquez had an exact copy made of the document, and, keeping the original, handed it over to them after due comparison, so that they could communicate with the prisoner.

Then, making an appointment for the morrow, they retired, and, not wishing to lose an instant in seeing Joam Dacosta, they hastened on to the prison; and there, in a short interview, informed him of all that had passed.

Joam Dacosta took the document and carefully examined it. Shaking his head, he handed it back to his son. "Perhaps," he said, "there is therein written the proof I shall never be able to produce. But if that proof escapes me, if the whole tenor of my life does not plead for me, I have nothing more to expect from the justice of men, and my fate is in the hands of God!"

And all felt it to be so. If the document remained indecipherable, the position of the convict was a desperate one.

"We shall find it, father!" exclaimed Benito.

"There never was a document of this sort yet which could stand examination. Have confidence—yes, confidence! Heaven has, so to speak, miraculously given us the paper which vindicates you, and, after guiding our hands to recover it, it will not refuse to direct our brains to unravel it."

Joam Dacosta shook hands with Benito and Manoel, and then the three young men, much agitated, retired to the jangada, where Yaquita was awaiting them.

Yaquita was soon informed of what had happened since the evening—the reappearance of the body of Torres, the discovery of the document, and the strange form under which the real culprit, the companion of the adventurer, had thought proper to write his confession—doubtless, so that it should not compromise him if it fell into strange hands.

Naturally, Lina was informed of this unexpected complication, and of the discovery made by Fragoso, that Torres was an old captain of the woods belonging to the gang who were employed about the mouths of the Madeira.

"But under what circumstances did you meet him?" asked the young mulatto.

"It was during one of my runs across the province of Amazones," replied Fragoso, "when I was going from village to village, working at my trade."

"And the scar?"

"What happened was this: One day I arrived at the mission of Aranas at the moment that Torres, whom I had never before seen, had picked a quarrel with one of his comrades—and a bad lot they are! and this quarrel ended with a stab from a knife, which entered the arm of the captain of the woods. There was no doctor there, and so I took charge of the wound, and that is how I made his acquaintance."

"What does it matter, after all," replied the young girl, "that we know what Torres had been? He was not the author of the crime, and it does not help us in the least."

"No, it does not," answered Fragoso; "for we

shall end by reading this document, and then the innocence of Joam Dacosta will be palpable to the eyes of all."

This was likewise the hope of Yaquita, of Benito, of Manoel, and of Minha, and, shut up in the house, they passed long hours in endeavoring to decipher the writing.

But if it was their hope—and there is no need to insist on that point—it was none the less that of Judge Jarriquez.

After having drawn up his report at the end of his examination establishing the identity of Joam Dacosta, the magistrate had sent it off to head-quarters, and therewith he thought he had finished with the affair so far as he was concerned. It could not well be otherwise.

On the discovery of the document, Jarriquez suddenly found himself face to face with the study of which he was a master. He, the seeker after numerical combinations, the solver of amusing problems, the answerer of charades, rebuses, logogryphs, and such things, was at last in his true element.

At the thought that the document might perhaps contain the justification of Joam Dacosta, he felt all the instinct of an analyst aroused. Here, before his very eyes, was a cryptogram ! And so from that moment he thought of nothing but how to discover its meaning, and it is scarcely necessary to say that he made up his mind to work at it continuously, even if he forgot to eat or to drink.

After the departure of the young people, Judge Jarriquez installed himself in his study. His door, barred against every one, assured him of several hours of perfect solitude. His spectacles were on his nose, his snuff-box on the table. He took a good pinch so as to develop the finesse and sagacity of his mind. He picked up the document and became absorbed in meditation, which soon became materialized in the shape of a monologue. The worthy justice was one of those unreserved men who think more easily aloud than to himself. "Let us proceed with method," he said. "No method, no logic ; no logic, no success."

Then, taking the document, he ran through it from beginning to end, without understanding it in the least.

The document contained a hundred lines, which were divided into half a dozen paragraphs.

"Hum !" said the judge, after a little reflection ; "to try every paragraph, one after the other, would be to lose precious time, and be of no use. I had better select one of these paragraphs, and take the one which is likely to prove the most interesting. Which of them would do this better than the last, where the recital of the whole affair is probably summed up ? Proper names might put me on the track, among others that of Joam Dacosta ; and if he has anything to do with this document, his name will evidently not be absent from its concluding paragraph."

The magistrate's reasoning was logical, and he was decidedly right in bringing all his resources to bear in the first place on the gist of the cryptogram as contained in its last paragraph.

Here is the paragraph, for it is necessary to again bring it before the eyes of the reader so as to show how an analyst set to work to discover its meaning.

"*P h y j s l y d d q f d z x g a s g z z q q e h x g k f n d r x u j u g i o c y t d x v k s b x h h u y p o h d v y r y m h u h p u y d k j o x p h e t o z s l e t n p m v ff o v p d p a j x h y n o j y g g a y m e q y n f u q l n m v l y f g s u z m q i z t l b q g y u g s q e u b v n r c r e d g r u z b l r m x y u h q h p z d r r g c r o h e p q x u f i v v r p l p h o n t h v d d q f h q s n t z h h h n f e p m q k y u u e x k t o g z g k y u u m f v i j d q d p z j q s y k r p l x h x q r y m v k l o h h h o t o z v d k s p p s u v j h d.*"

At the outset, Judge Jarriquez noticed that the lines of the document were not divided either into words or phrases, and that there was a complete absence of punctuation. This fact could but render the reading of the document more difficult.

"Let me see, however," he said, "if there is not some assemblage of the letters which appears to form a word—I mean a pronounceable word, whose number of consonants is in proportion to its vowels. And at the beginning I see the word *phy*; farther on the word *gas*. Hallo! *ujugi*. Does this mean the African town on the banks of Tanganyika! What has this got to do with all this? Farther on here is the word *ypo*. Is it Greek, then? Close by here is *rym* and *puy*, and *jox*, and *phetoz*, and *jyggay*, and *mv*, and *qruz*. And before that we had got *rcd* and *let*. That is good! those are two English words. Then *ohe—syk*; then *rym* once more, and then the word *oto*."

Judge Jarriquez let the paper drop, and thought for a few minutes.

"All the words I see in this thing seem queer!" he said. "In fact, there is nothing to give a clue to their origin. Some look like Greek, some like Dutch; some have an English twist, and some look like nothing at all! To say nothing of these series of consonants which are not wanted in any human pronunciation. Most assuredly it would not be very easy to find the key to this cryptogram."

The magistrate's fingers commenced to beat a tattoo on his desk—a kind of reveille to arouse his dormant faculties.

"Let us see," he said, "how many letters there are in the paragraph."

He then counted them, pen in hand.

"Two hundred and seventy-six!" he said. "Well, now let us try what proportion these different letters bear to each other."

This occupied him for some time. The judge took up the document, and, with his pen in his hand, he noted each letter in alphabetical order.

In a quarter of an hour he had obtained the follow.
ing table :—

$$
\begin{array}{rcl}
a &=& 3 \ \text{times.} \\
b &=& 4 \ — \\
c &=& 3 \ — \\
d &=& 16 \ — \\
e &=& 9 \ — \\
f &=& 10 \ — \\
g &=& 13 \ — \\
h &=& 23 \ — \\
i &=& 4 \ — \\
j &=& 8 \ — \\
k &=& 9 \ — \\
l &=& 9 \ — \\
m &=& 9 \ — \\
n &=& 9 \ — \\
o &=& 12 \ — \\
p &=& 16 \ — \\
q &=& 16 \ — \\
r &=& 12 \ — \\
s &=& 10 \ — \\
t &=& 8 \ — \\
u &=& 17 \ — \\
v &=& 13 \ — \\
x &=& 12 \ — \\
y &=& 19 \ — \\
z &=& 12 \ — \\
\end{array}
$$

Total . . . . . 276 times.

"Ah, ah!" he exclaimed. "One thing strikes me at
once, and that is that in this paragraph all the letters
of the alphabet are not used. This is very strange. If
we take up a book and open it by chance it will be
very seldom that we hit upon two hundred and seventy-six letters without all the signs of the alphabet
figuring among them. After all, it may be chance,"
and then he passed to a different train of thought.
"One important point is to see if the vowels and consonants are in their normal proportion."

And so he seized his pen, counted up the vowels, and obtained the following result:—

$$a = 3 \text{ times.}$$
$$e = 9 \text{ —}$$
$$i = 4 \text{ —}$$
$$o = 12 \text{ —}$$
$$u = 17 \text{ —}$$
$$y = 19 \text{ —}$$

Total . . . . . 64 vowels.

"And thus there are in this paragraph, after we have done our subtraction, sixty-four vowels and two hundred and twelve consonants. Good! that is the normal proportion. That is about a fifth, as in the alphabet, where there are six vowels among twenty-six letters. It is possible, therefore, that the document is written in the language of our country, and that only the signification of each letter is changed. If it has been modified in regular order, and a *b* is always represented by an *l*, an *o* by a *v*, a *g* by a *k*, an *u* by an *r*, etc., I will give up my judgeship if I do not read it. What can I do better than follow the method of that great analytical genius, Edgar Allan Poe?"

Judge Jarriquez herein alluded to a story by the great American romancer, which is a masterpiece. Who has not read the "Gold Bug"? In this novel a cryptogram, composed of ciphers, letters, algebraic signs, asterisks, full-stops, and commas, is submitted to a truly mathematical analysis, and is deciphered under extraordinary conditions, which the admirers of that strange genius can never forget. On the reading of the American document depended only a treasure, while on that of this one depended a man's life. Its solution was consequently all the more interesting.

The magistrate, who had often read and re-read his

"Gold Bug," was perfectly acquainted with the steps in the analysis so minutely described by Edgar Poe, and he resolved to proceed in the same way on this occasion. In doing so he was certain, as he had said, that if the value or signification of each letter remained constant, he would, sooner or later, arrive at the solution of the document.

"What did Edgar Poe do?" he repeated. "First of all he began by finding out the sign—here there are only letters, let us say the letter—which was reproduced the oftenest. I see that that is *h*, for it is met with twenty-three times. This enormous proportion shows, to begin with, that *h* does not stand for *h*, but, on the contrary, that it represents the letter which recurs most frequently in our language, for I suppose the document is written in Portuguese. In English or French it would certainly be *e*, in Italian it would be *i* or *a*, in Portuguese it will be *a* or *o*. Now let us say that *h* signifies *a* or *o*."

After this was done, the judge found out the letter which recurred most frequently after *h*, and so on, and he formed the following table:—

| | | |
|---|---|---|
| *h* | = 23 | times. |
| *y* | = 19 | — |
| *u* | = 17 | — |
| *d p q* | = 16 | — |
| *g v* | = 13 | — |
| *o r x z* | = 12 | — |
| *f s* | = 10 | — |
| *e k l m n* | = 9 | — |
| *j t* | = 8 | — |
| *b i* | = 4 | — |
| *a c* | = 3 | — |

"Now the letter *a* only occurs thrice!" exclaimed the judge, "and it ought to occur the oftenest. Ah! that clearly proves that the meaning has been changed. And now, after *a* or *o*, what are the letters which figure oftenest in our language? Let us see," and Judge Jarriquez, with truly remarkable sagacity, which de-

noted a very observant mind, started on this new quest.
In this he was only imitating the American romancer,
who, great analyst as he was, had, by simple induction,
been able to construct an alphabet corresponding to
the signs of the cryptogram, and by means of it to
eventually read the pirate's parchment note with ease.

The magistrate set to work in the same way, and we
may affirm that he was no whit inferior to his illustri-
ous master. Thanks to his previous work at logogryphs and squares, rectangular arrangements, and
other enigmas, which depend only on an arbitrary disposition of the letters, he was already pretty strong in
such mental pastimes. On this occasion he sought to
establish the order in which the letters were reproduced—vowels first, consonants afterwards.

Three hours had elapsed since he began. He had
before his eyes an alphabet which, if his procedure
were right, would give him the right meaning of the
letters in the document. He had only to successively
apply the letters of his alphabet to those of his paragraph. But before making this application some
slight emotion seized upon the judge. He fully experienced the intellectual gratification—much greater
than, perhaps, would be thought—of the man who,
after hours of obstinate endeavor, saw the impatiently
sought-for sense of the logogryph coming into view.

"Now let us try," he said; "and I shall be very
much surprised if I have not got the solution of the
enigma!"

Judge Jarriquez took off his spectacles and wiped
the glasses; then he put them back again, and bent
over the table. His special alphabet was in one hand,
the cryptogram in the other. He commenced to write
under the first line of the paragraph the true letters,
which, according to him, ought to correspond exactly
with each of the cryptographic letters. As with the
first line so did he with the second, and the third, and
the fourth, until he had reached the end of the paragraph.

Oddity as he was, he did not stop to see as he wrote
if the assemblage of letters made intelligible words.

No; during the first stage his mind refused all verification of that sort. What he desired was to give himself the ecstasy of reading it all straight off at once.

And now he had done.

"Let us read!" he exclaimed.

And he read. Good heavens! what cacophony! The lines he had formed with the letters of his alphabet had no more sense in them than those of the document! It was another series of letters, and that was all They formed no word; they had no value. In short, they were just as hieroglyphic.

"Confound the thing!" exclaimed Judge Jarriquez.

---

## CHAPTER XIII.

### IS IT A MATTER OF FIGURES?

IT was seven o'clock in the evening. Judge Jarriquez had all the time been absorbed in working at the puzzle—and was no further advanced—and had forgotten the time of repast and the time of repose, when there came a knock at his study door.

It was time. An hour later, and all the cerebral substance of the vexed magistrate would certainly have evaporated under the intense heat into which he had worked his head.

At the order to enter—which was given in an impatient tone—the door opened and Manoel presented himself.

The young doctor had left his friends on board the jaganda at work on the indecipherable document, and had come to see Judge Jarriquez. He was anxious to know if he had been fortunate in his researches. He had come to ask if he had at length discovered the system on which the cryptogram had been written.

The magistrate was not sorry to see Manoel come in. He was in that state of excitement that solitude was exasperating to him. He wanted some one to

6

speak to, some one as anxious to penetrate the mystery as he was. Manoel was just the man.

"Sir," said Manoel, as he entered, "one question! Have you succeeded better than we have?"

"Sit down first," exclaimed Judge Jarriquez, who got up and began to pace the room. "Sit down! If we are both of us standing, you will walk one way and I shall walk the other, and the room will be too narrow to hold us."

Manoel sat down and repeated his question.

"No! I have not had any success!" replied the magistrate; "I do not think I am any better off. I have got nothing to tell you; but I have found out a certainty."

"What is that, sir?"

"That the document is not based on conventional signs, but on what is known in cryptology as a cipher, that is to say, on a number."

"Well, sir," answered Manoel, "cannot a document of that kind always be read?"

"Yes," said Jarriquez, "if a letter is invariably represented by the same letter; if an *a*, for example, is always a *p*, and a *p* is always an *x;* if not, it cannot."

"And in this document?"

"In this document the value of the letter changes with the arbitrarily selected cipher which necessitates it. So a *b* which will in one place be represented by a *k* will later on become a *z*, later on a *u* or an *n* or an *f* or any other letter." "And then?"

"And then, I am sorry to say, the cryptogram is indecipherable."

"Indecipherable!" exclaimed Manoel. "No, sir; we shall end by finding the key of the document on which the man's life depends."

Manoel had risen, a prey to the excitement he could not control; the reply he had received was too hopeless, and he refused to accept it for good.

At a gesture from the judge, however, he sat down again, and in a calmer voice asked:

"And in the first place, sir, what makes you think that the basis of this document is a number, or, as you call it, a cipher?"

"Listen to me, young man," replied the judge, "and you will be forced to give in to the evidence."

The magistrate took the document and put it before the eyes of Manoel and showed him what he had done.

"I began," he said, "by treating this document in the proper way, that is to say, logically, leaving nothing to chance. I applied to it an alphabet based on the proportion the letters bear to one another which is usual in our language, and I sought to obtain the meaning by following the precepts of our immortal analyst, Edgar Poe. Well, what succeeded with him collapsed with me."

"Collapsed!" exclaimed Manoel.

"Yes, my dear young man, and I at once saw that success sought in that fashion was impossible. In truth, a stronger man than I might have been deceived."

"But I should like to understand," said Manoel, "and I do not——"

"Take the document," continued Judge Jarriquez; "first look at the disposition of the letters, and read it through."

Manoel obeyed.

"Do you not see that the combination of several of the letters is very strange?" asked the magistrate.

"I do not see anything," said Manoel, after having for perhaps the hundredth time read through the document.

"Well! study the last paragraph! There you understand the sense of the whole is bound to be summed up. Do you see anything abnormal?"

"Nothing."

"There is, however, one thing which absolutely proves that the language is subject to the laws of number."

"And that is?"

"That is that you see three *h's* coming together in two different places."

What Jarriquez said was correct, and it was of a nature to attract attention. The two hundred and fourth, two hundred and fifth, and two hundred and sixth letters of the paragraph, and the two hundred and fifty-eighth, two hundred and fifty-ninth, and two hundred and sixtieth letters of the paragraph, were consecutive *h's.* At first this peculiarity had not struck the magistrate.

"And that proves?" asked Manoel, without divining the deduction that could be drawn from the combination.

"That simply proves that the basis of the document is a number. It shows *a priori* that each letter is modified in virtue of the ciphers of the number and according to the place which it occupies."

"And why?"

"Because in no language will you find words with three consecutive repetitions of the letter *h.*"

Manoel was struck with the argument; he thought about it, and, in short, had no reply to make.

"And had I made the observation sooner," continued the magistrate, "I might have spared myself a good deal of trouble and a headache which extends from my occiput to my sinciput."

"But, sir," asked Manoel, who felt the little hope vanishing on which he had hitherto rested, "what do you mean by a cipher?"

"Tell me a number."

"Any number you like."

"Give me an example and you will understand the explanation better."

Judge Jarriquez sat down at the table, took up a sheet of paper and a pencil, and said:

"Now, Mr. Manoel, let us choose a sentence by chance, the first that comes; for instance——

*Judge Jarrequez has an ingenious mind.*

I write this phrase so as to space the letters differently, and I get—

*Judgejarrequezhasaningeniousmind.*

That done," said the magistrate, to whom the phrase seemed to contain a proposition beyond dispute, looking Manoel straight in the face, "suppose I take a number by chance, so as to give a cryptographic form to this natural succession of words; suppose now

this word is composed of three ciphers, and let these
ciphers be 2, 3 and 4.   Now on the line below I put
the number 234, and   repeat it as many times as are
necessary to get to the end of the phrase, and so that
every cipher comes underneath a letter.   This is what
we get—

*J u d g e j   a r r i q u e z h a s a n i n g e n i o u s m i n d.*
² 3 4 ² 3 4   ² 3 4 ² 3 4 ² 3   4 ² 3 4 ²   3 4 ²   3 4 ² 3 4 ² 3 4 ² 3

And now, Mr. Manoel, replacing each letter by the letter in advance of it in alphabetical order according to
the value of the cipher, we get—

*j* plus 2 equal *l*

*u* plus 3 equal *x*

*d* plus 4 equal *h*

*g* plus 2 equal *i*

*e* plus 3 equal *h*

*j* plus 4 equal *n*

*a* plus 2 equal *c*

*r* plus 3 equal *u*

*r* plus 4 equal *v*

*i* plus 2 equal *k*

*q* plus 3 equal *t*

*u* plus 4 equal *y*

*e* plus 2 equal *g*

*z* plus 3 equal *c*

*h* plus 4 equal *t*

*a* plus 2 equal *c*

*s* plus 3 equal *v*

*a* plus 4 equal *e*

*n* plus 2 equal *p*

*i* plus 3 equal *l*

*n* plus 4 equal *r*

*g* plus 2 equal *i*

*e* plus 3 equal *h*

*n* plus 4 equal *r*

*i* plus 2 equal *k*

*o* plus 3 equal *r*

*u* plus 4 equal *y*

*s* plus 2 equal *u*

and so on.

"If, on account of the value of the ciphers which compose the number, I come to the end of the alphabet without having enough complementary letters to deduct, I begin again at the beginning. That is what happens at the end of my name when the *z* is replaced by the 3. As after *z* the alphabet has no more letters, I commence to count from *a* and so get the *c*. That done, when I get to the end of this cryptographic system, made up of the 234—which was arbitrarily selected, do not forget!—the phrase which you recognize above is replaced by—

*lxhihncuvktygclcveplrihrkryupmpg.*

"And now, young man, just look at it, and do you not think it is very much like what is in the document? Well, what is the consequence? Why, that the signification of the letters depends on a cipher which chance put beneath them, and the cryptographic letter which answers to a true one is not always the same. So in this phrase the first *j* is represented by an *l*, the second by an *n;* the first *e* by an *h*, the second by a *g*, the third by an *h;* the first *d* is represented by an *h*, the last by a *g ;* the first *u* by an *x*, the last by a *y ;* the first and second *a's* by a *c*, the last by an *e;* and in my own name one *r* is represented by a *u*, the other by a *v*, and so on. Now you see that if you do not know the cipher 234 you will never be able to read the lines, and consequently if we do not know the number of the document, it remains undecipherable !"

On hearing the magistrate reason with such careful logic, Manoel was at first overwhelmed, but, raising his head, he exclaimed :

"No, sir, I will not renounce the hope of finding the number !"

"We might have done so," answered Judge Jarriquez, "if the lines of the document had been divided into words."

"And why ?"

"For this reason, young man. I think we can assnme that in the last paragraph all that is written in these earlier paragraphs is summed up. Now I am

convinced that in it will be found the name of Joam
Dacosta. Well, if the lines had been divided into
words, in trying the words one after the other—I mean
the words composed of seven letters, as the name of
Dacosta is—it would not have been impossible to
evolve the number which is the key of the document.

"Will you explain to me how you ought to proceed
to do that, sir?" asked Manoel, who probably caught a
glimpse of one more hope.

"Nothing can be more simple," answered the judge.
"Let us take, for example, one of the words in the sentence we have just written—my name, if you like. It
is represented in the cryptogram by this queer succession of letters, *ncuvktygc*. Well, arranging these letters
in a column, one under the other, and then placing
them against the letters of my name, and deducting
one from the other the numbers of their places in alphabetical order, I get the following result:

$$\text{Between } n \text{ and } j \text{ we have } 4 \text{ letters}$$

| | | | | | |
|---|---|---|---|---|---|
| — | $c$ | — $a$ | — | 2 | — |
| — | $u$ | — $r$ | — | 3 | — |
| — | $v$ | — $r$ | — | 4 | — |
| — | $k$ | — $i$ | — | 2 | — |
| — | $t$ | — $q$ | — | 3 | — |
| — | $y$ | — $u$ | — | 4 | — |
| — | $g$ | — $e$ | — | 2 | — |
| — | $c$ | — $z$ | — | 3 | — |

"Now what is the column of ciphers made up of
that we have got by this simple operation? Look
here! 423, 423, 423, that is to say, of repetitions of the
numbers 423, or 234, or 342."

"Yes, that is it!" answered Manoel.

"You understand, then, by this means, that in cal-
culating the true letter from the false, instead of the
false from the true, I have been able to discover the
number with ease; and the number I was in search of
is really the 234 which I took as the key to my cryptogram."

"Well, sir!" exclaimed Manoel, "if that is so, the

name of Dacosta is in the last paragraph; and taking successively each letter of these lines for the first of the seven letters which compose his name, we ought to get ——"

"That would be impossible," interrupted the judge, "except on one condition."

"What is that?"

"That the first cipher of the number should happen to be the first letter of the word Dacosta, and I think you will agree with me that it is not probable."

"Quite so!" sighed Manoel, who, with this improbability, saw the last chance vanish.

"And so we must trust to chance alone," continued Jarriquez, who shook his head, "and chance does not often do much in things of this sort."

"But still," said Manoel, "chance might give us this number."

"This number," exclaimed the magistrate—"this number? But how many ciphers is it composed of? Of two, or three, or four, or nine, or ten? Is it made up of different ciphers only, or of ciphers in different order many times repeated? Do you not know, young man, that with the ordinary ten ciphers, using all at a time, but without any repetition, you can make 3,268,-800 different numbers, and that if you use the same cipher more than once in the number, these millions of combinations will be enormously increased? And do you not know that if we employ every one of the 525,600 minutes of which the year is composed to try at each of these numbers, it would take you six years, and that you would want three centuries if each operation took you an hour? No! You ask the impossible!"

"Impossible, sir?" answered Manoel. "An innocent man has been branded as guilty, and Joam Dacosta is to lose his life and his honor while you hold in your hands the material proof of his innocence. That is what is impossible!"

"Ah, young man!" exclaimed Jarriquez, "who told you, after all, that Torres did not tell a lie? Who told you that he really did have in his hands a document

written by the author of the crime? that this paper
was the document, and that this document refers to
Joam Dacosta?"

"Who told me so?" repeated Manoel, and his face
was hidden in his hands.

In fact, nothing could prove for certain that the
document had anything to do with the affair in the
diamond province. There was, in fact, nothing to
show that it was not utterly devoid of meaning, and
that it had been imagined by Torres himself, who was
as capable of selling a false thing as a true one!

"It does not matter, Manoel," continued the judge,
rising; "it does not matter! Whatever it may be to
which the document refers, I have not yet given up
discovering the cipher. After all, it is worth more
than a logogryph or a rebus!"

At these words Manoel rose, shook hands with
the magistrate, and returned to the jangada, feeling more hopeless when he went back than when
he set out.

---

## CHAPTER XIV.

### CHANCE !

A COMPLETE change took place in public opinion
on the subject of Joam Dacosta. To anger succeeded pity. The population no longer thronged to
the prison of Manaos to roar out cries of death to the
prisoner. On the contrary, the most forward of them
in accusing him of being the principal author of the
crime of Tijuco now averred that he was not guilty,
and demanded his immediate restoration to liberty.
Thus it always is with the mob—from one extreme
they run to the other. But the change was intelligible.

The events which had happened in the last few days
—the struggle between Benito and Torres; the search
for the corpse, which had reappeared under such extraordinary circumstances; the finding of the "inde-

cipherable " document, if we can so call it; the information it concealed, the assurance that it contained,
or rather the wish that it contained, the material
proof of the guiltlessness of Joam Dacosta; and the hope
that it was written by the real culprit—all these things
had contributed to work the change in public opinion.
What the people had desired and impatiently demanded forty-eight hours before, they now feared, and
that was the arrival of the instructions due from Rio
de Janeiro.

These, however, were not likely to be delayed.

Joam Dacosta had been arrested on the 24th of
August, and examined next day. The judge's report
was sent off on the 26th. It was now the 28th. In
three or four days more the Minister would have come
to a decision regarding the convict, and it was only
too certain that justice would take its course.

There was no doubt that such would be the case.
On the other hand, that the assurance of Dacosta's innocence would appear from the document, was not
doubted by anybody, neither by his family nor by the
fickle population of Manaos, who excitedly followed
the phases of this dramatic affair.

But, on the other hand, in the eyes of disinterested
or indifferent persons who were not affected by the
event, what value could be assigned to this document ?
and how could they even declare that it referred to
the crime in the diamond arrayal ? It existed, that
was undeniable; it had been found on the corpse of
Torres, nothing could be more certain. It could even
be seen, by comparing it with the letter in which Torres
gave the information about Joam Dacosta, that the
document was not in the handwriting of the adventurer. But, as had been suggested by Judge Jarriquez, why should not the scoundrel have invented it
for the sake of his bargain ? And this was less unlikely to be the case, considering that Torres had declined
to part with it until after his marriage with Dacosta's
daughter—that is to say, when it would have been impossible to undo an accomplished fact.

All these views were held by some people in some

form, and we can quite understand what interest the affair created. In any case, the situation of Joam Dacosta was most hazardous. If the document were not deciphered, it would be just the same as if it did not exist; and if the secret of the cryptogram were not miraculously divined or revealed before the end of the three days, the supreme sentence would inevitably be suffered by the doomed man of Tijuco. And this miracle a man attempted to perform! The man was Jarriquez, and he now really set to work more in the interest of Joam Dacosta than for the satisfaction of his analytical faculties. A complete change had also taken place in his opinion. Was not this man, who had voluntarily abandoned his retreat at Iquitos, who had come at the risk of his life to demand his rehabilitation at the hands of Brazilian justice, a moral enigma worth all the others put together? And so the judge had resolved never to leave the document until he had discovered the cipher. He set to work at it in a fury. He ate no more; he slept no more! All his time was passed in inventing combinations of numbers, in forging a key to force this lock!

This idea had taken possession of Judge Jarriquez's brain at the end of the first day. Suppressed frenzy consumed him, and kept him in a perpetual heat. His whole house trembled; his servants, black or white, dared not come near him. Fortunately he was a bachelor; had there been a Madame Jarriquez she would have had a very uncomfortable time of it. Never had a problem so taken possession of this oddity, and he had thoroughly made up his mind to get at the solution, even if his head exploded like an overheated boiler under the tension of its vapor.

It was perfectly clear to the mind of the worthy magistrate that the key to the document was a number, composed of two or more ciphers, but what this number was all investigation seemed powerless to discover.

This was the enterprise on which Jarriquez, in quite a fury, was engaged, and during this 28th of August he brought all his faculties to bear on it, and worked away almost superhumanly.

To arrive at the number by chance, he said, was to lose himself in millions of combinations, which would absorb the life of a first-rate calculator. But if he could in no respect reckon on chance, was it impossible to proceed by reasoning? Decidedly not! And so it was "to reason till he became unreasoning" that Judge Jarriquez gave himself up after vainly seeking repose in a few hours of sleep. He who ventured in upon him at this moment after braving the formal defenses which protected his solitude, would have found him, as on the day before, in his study, before his desk, with the document under his eyes, the thousands of letters of which seemed all jumbled together and flying about his head.

"Ah!" he exclaimed, "why did not the scoundrel who wrote this separate the words in this paragraph? We might—we will try—but no! However, if there is anything here about the murder and the robbery, two or three words there must be in it—'arrayal,' 'diamond,' 'Tijuco,' 'Dacosta,' and others; and in putting down their cryptological equivalents the number could be arrived at. But there is nothing—not a break!—not one word by itself! One word of two hundred and seventy-six letters! I hope the wretch may be blessed two hundred and seventy-six times for complicating his system in this way! He ought to be hanged two hundred and seventy-six times!"

And a violent thump with his fist on the document emphasized this charitable wish.

"But," continued the magistrate, "if I cannot find one of the words in the body of the document, I might at least try my hand at the beginning and end of each paragraph. There may be a chance there that I ought not to miss."

And impressed with this idea Judge Jarriquez successively tried if the letters which commenced or finished the different paragraphs could be made to correspond with those which formed the most important word, which was sure to be found somewhere, that of *Dacosta*.

He could do nothing of the kind.

It fact, to take only the last paragraph with which he began, the formula was——

$$
\begin{aligned}
P &= D \\
h &= a \\
y &= c \\
j &= o \\
s &= s \\
l &= t \\
y &= a
\end{aligned}
$$

Now at the very first letter Jarriquez was stopped in his calculations, for the difference in alphabetical position between the $d$ and the $p$ gave him not one cipher but two, namely: 12, and in this kind of cryptogram only one letter can take the place of another.

It was the same for the seven last letters of the paragraph, $p \, s \, u \, v \, j \, h \, d$, of which the series also commences with a $p$, and which could in no case stand for the $d$ in *Dacosta*, because these letters were in like manner twelve spaces apart.

So it was not his name that figured here.

The same observation applied to the words *arrayal* and *Tijuco*, which were successively tried, but whose construction did not correspond with the cryptographic series.

After he had got so far, Judge Jarriquez, with his head nearly splitting, arose and paced his office, went for fresh air to the window, and gave utterance to a growl, at the noise of which a flock of humming-birds, murmuring among the foliage of a mimosa-tree, betook themselves to flight. Then he returned to the document.

He picked it up and turned it over.

"The humbug! the rascal!" he hissed; "it will end by driving me mad! But steady! Be calm! Don't let our spirits go down! This is not the time!"

And then having refreshed himself by giving his head a thorough sluicing with cold water.—

"Let us try another way," he said, "and as I cannot hit upon the number from the arrangement of the let-

ters, let us see what number the author of the document would have chosen in confessing that he was the
author of the crime at Tijuco."

This was another method for the magistrate to enter upon, and maybe he was right, for there was a
certain amount of logic about it.

"And first let us try a date. Why should not the
culprit have taken the date of the year in which Dacosta, the innocent man he allowed to be sentenced
in his place, was born? Was he likely to forget a number which was so important to him? Then Joam
Dacosta was born in 1804. Let us see what 1804 will
give us as a cryptological number."

And Judge Jarriquez wrote the first letters of the
paragraph, and putting over them the number 1804
repeated thrice, he obtained

$$1804 \qquad 1804 \qquad 1804$$
$$phyj \quad slyd \quad aqfd$$

Then in counting up the spaces in alphabetical order
he obtained

$$o.yf \quad rdy. \quad cif.$$

And this was meaningless! And he wanted three letters which he had to replace by points, because the
ciphers, 8, 4, and 4, which command the three letters,
*h*, *d*, and *d*, do not give corresponding letters in ascending the series.

"That is not it again!" exclaimed Jarriquez. "Let
us try another number."

And he asked himself, if instead of this first date
the author of the document had not rather selected
the date of the year in which the crime was committed.

This was in 1826.

And so proceeding as above, he obtained

$$1826 \qquad 1826 \qquad 1826$$
$$phyj \quad slyd \quad dqfd$$

and that gave

$$o.vd \quad rdv. \quad cid.$$

the same meaningless series, the same absence of sense, as many letters wanting as in the former instance, and for the same reason.

"Bother the number!" exclaimed the magistrate. "We must give it up again. Let us have another one! Perhaps the rascal chose the number of contos representing the amount of the booty!"

Now the value of the stolen diamonds was estimated at eight hundred and thirty-four contos, or about 2,500,000 francs, and so the formula became

$$\begin{array}{cccc} 8\,3\,4 & 8\,3\,4 & 8\,3\,4 & 8\,3\,4 \\ p\,h\,y & j\,s\,l & y\,d\,d & q\,f\,d \end{array}$$

and this gave a result as little gratifying as the others—

$$h\,e\,t \qquad b\,p\,h \qquad p\,a. \qquad i\,c.$$

"Confound the document and him who imagined it!" shouted Jarriquez, throwing down the paper, which was wafted to the other side of the room. "It would try the patience of a saint!"

But the short burst of anger passed away, and the magistrate, who had no idea of being beaten, picked up the paper. What he had done with the first letters of the different paragraphs he did with the last—and to no purpose. Then he tried everything his excited imagination could suggest.

He tried in succession the numbers which represented Dacosta's age, which should have been known to the author of the crime, the date of his arrest, the date of the sentence at the Villa Rica assizes, the date fixed for the execution, etc., etc., even the number of victims at the affray at Tijuco!

Nothing! All the time nothing!

Judge Jarriquez had worked himself into such a state of exasperation that there really was some fear that his mental faculties would lose their balance. He jumped about, and twisted about, and wrestled about as if he really had got hold of his enemy's body. Then suddenly he cried: "Now for chance! Heaven help me now, logic is powerless!"

His hand seized a bell-pull hanging near his table. The bell rang furiously, and the magistrate strode up to the door, which he opened. "Bobo !" he shouted.

A moment or two elapsed.

Bobo was a freed negro, who was the privileged servant of Jarriquez. He did not appear; it was evident that Bobo was afraid to come into his master's room.

Another ring at the bell; another call to Bobo, who, for his own safety, pretended to be deaf on this occasion. And now a third ring at the bell, which unhitched the crank and broke the cord.

This time Bobo came up. "What is it, sir ?" asked Bobo, prudently waiting on the threshold.

"Advance, without uttering a single word!" replied the judge, whose flaming eyes made the negro quake again.

Bobo advanced.

"Bobo," said Jarriquez, "attend to what I say, and answer immediately; do not even take time to think, or I——"

Bobo, with fixed eyes and open mouth, brought his feet together like a soldier and stood at attention.

"Are you ready ?" asked his master.

"I am."

"Now, then, tell me, without a moment's thought— you understand—the first number that comes into your head."

"76223," answered Bobo, all in a breath. Bobo thought he would please his master by giving him a pretty large one!

Judge Jarriquez had run to the table, and, pencil in hand, had made out a formula with the number given by Bobo, and which Bobo had in his way only given him at a venture.

It is obvious that it was most unlikely that a number such as 76223 was the key of the document, and it produced no other result than to bring to the lips of Jarriquez such a vigorous ejaculation that Bobo disappeared like a shot!

## CHAPTER XV.

### THE LAST EFFORT.

THE magistrate, however, was not the only one who
passed his time unprofitably. Benito, Manoel,
Minha tried all they could together to extract the
secret from the document on which depended their
father's life and honor. On his part, Fragoso, aided
by Lina, could not remain quiet, but all their ingenuity
had failed, and the number still escaped them.

" Why don't you find it, Fragoso?" asked the young
mulatto.

" I will find it," answered Fragoso.

And he did not find it!

Here we should say that Fragoso had an idea of a
project of which he had not even spoken to Lina, but
which had taken full possession of his mind. This
was to go in search of the gang to which the ex-captain
of the woods had belonged, and to find out who was
the probable author of this cipher document, which
was supposed to be the confession of the culprit of
Tijuco. The part of the Amazon where these people
were employed, the very place where Fragoso had met
Torres a few years before, was not very far from
Manaos. He would only have to descend the river
for about fifty miles, to the mouth of the Madeira, a
tributary coming in on the right, and there he was
almost sure to meet the head of these " capitaes do
mato," to which Torres belonged. In two days, or
three days at the outside, Fragoso could get into communication with the old comrades of the adventurer.

" Yes! I could do that," he repeated to himself;
" but what would be the good of it, supposing I succeeded? If we are sure that one of Torres' companions

7

has recently died, would that prove him to be the
author of this crime? Would that show that he gave
Torres a document in which he announced himself the
author of this crime, and exonerated Joam Dacosta?
Would this give us the key of the document? No!
Two men only knew the cipher—the culprit and
Torres ! And these two men are no more!"

So reasoned Fragoso. It was evident that his enterprise would do no good. But the thought of it
was too much for him. An irresistible influence im-
pelled him to set out, although he was not even sure
of finding the band on the Madeira. In fact, it might
be engaged in some other part of the province, and to
come up with it might require more time than Fragoso had at his disposal! And what would be the
result?

It is none the less true, however, that on the 29th
of August, before sunrise, Fragoso, without saying
anything to anybody, secretly left the jangada, arrived
at Manaos, and embarked in one of the egariteas
which daily descend the Amazon.

And great was the astonishment when he was not
seen on board, and did not appear during the day.
No one, not even Lina, could explain the absence of
so devoted a servant at such a crisis.

Some of them even asked, and not without reason,
if the poor fellow, rendered desperate at having, when
he met him on the frontier, personally contributed to
bringing Torres on board the raft, had not made away
with himself.

But if Fragoso could so reproach himself, how about
Benito? In the first place, at Iquitos he had invited
Torres to visit the fazenda; in the second place, he had
brought him on board the jangada, to become a pas-
senger on it; and in the third place, in killing him, he
had annihilated the only witness whose evidence could
save the condemned man.

And so Benito considered himself responsible for
everything—the arrest of his father, and the terrible
events of which it had been the consequence.

In fact had Torres been alive, Benito could not tell

but that, in some way or another, from pity or for reward, he would have finished by handing over the
document. Would not Torres, whom nothing could
compromise, have been persuaded to speak, had money
been brought to bear upon him? Would not the long-
sought-for proof have been furnished to the judge?
Yes, undoubtedly! And the only man who could
have furnished this evidence had been killed through
Benito!

Such was what the wretched man continually repeated to his mother, to Manoel, and to himself;
were the cruel responsibilities which his conscience
laid to his charge.

Between her husband, with whom she passed all the
time that was allowed to her, and her son, a prey to
despair which made her tremble for his reason, the
brave Yaquita lost none of her moral energy. In
her they found the valiant daughter of Magalhaes, the
worthy wife of the fazender of Iquitos.

The attitude of Joam Dacosta was well adapted to
sustain her in this ordeal. That gallant man, that
rigid Puritan, that austere worker, whose whole life
had been a battle, had not yet shown a moment of
weakness.

The most terrible blow which had struck him with-
cut prostrating him had been the death of Judge Ribeiro, in whose mind his innocence did not admit of a
doubt. Was it not with the help of his old defender
that he had hoped to strive for his rehabilitation? The
intervention of Torres he had regarded throughout as
being quite secondary for him. And of this document he had no knowledge when he left Iquitos to
hand himself over to the justice of his country He
only took with him moral proofs. When a material
proof was unexpectedly produced in the course of the
affair, before or after his arrest, he was certainly not
the man to despise it. But if, on acccount of regret-
able circumstances, the proof disappeared, he would
find himself once more in the same position as when
he passed the Brazilian frontier—the position of a man
who came to say: "Here is my past life; here is my

present; here is an entirely honest existence of work and devotion which I bring you. You passed on me at first an erroneous judgment. After three and twenty years of exile I have come to give myself up! Here I am; judge me again!"

The death of Torres, the impossibility of reading the document found on him, had thus not produced on Joam Dacosta the impression which it had on his children, his friends, his household, and all who were interested in him.

"I have faith in my innocence," he repeated to Yaquita, "as I have faith in God. If my life is still useful to my people, and a miracle is necessary to save me, that miracle will be performed; if not, I shall die! God alone is my judge!"

The excitement increased in Manaos as the time ran on the affair was discussed with unexampled acerbity. In the midst of this enthralment of public opinion, which evoked so much of the mysterious, the document was the principal object of conversation.

At the end of this fourth day not a single person doubted but that it contained the vindication of the doomed man. Every one had been given an opportunity of deciphering its incomprehensible contents, for the "Diario d'o Grand Para" had reproduced it in facsimile. Autograph copies were spread about in great numbers at the suggestion of Manoel, who neglected nothing that might lead to the penetration of the mystery—not even chance, that "nickname of providence," as some one has called it.

In addition, a reward of 100 contos (or 300,000 francs) was promised to any one who could discover the cipher so fruitlessly sought after—and read the document. This was quite a fortune, and so people of all classes forgot to eat, drink, or sleep to attack this unintelligible cryptogram.

Up to the present, however, all had been useless, and probably the most ingenious analysts in the world would have spent their time in vain. It had been advertised that any solution should be sent, without delay, to Judge Jarriquez, to his house in God-the-Son

Street ; but the evening of the 29th of August came and none had arrived, nor was any likely to arrive.

Of all those who took up the study of the puzzle, Judge Jarriquez was one of the most to be pitied. By a natural association of ideas, he also joined in the general opinion that the document referred to the affair at Tijuco, and that it had been written by the hand of the guilty man, and exonerated Joam Dacosta. And so he put even more ardor into his search for the key. It was not only the art for the art's sake which guided him, it was a sentiment of justice, of pity toward a man suffering under an unjust condemnation. If it is the fact that a certain quantity of phosphorus is expended in the work of the brain, it would be difficult to say how many milligrammes the judge had parted with to excite the network of his " sensorium," and after all, to find out nothing, absolutely nothing.

But Jarriquez had no idea of abandoning the in-quiry. If he could only now trust to chance, he would work on for that chance. He tried to evoke it by all means possible and impossible. He had given himself over to fury and anger, and what was worse, to impotent anger!

During the latter part of this day he had been trying different numbers—numbers selected arbitrarily—and how many of them can scarcely be imagined. Had he had the time, he would not have shrunk from plunging into the millions of combinations of which the ten symbols of numeration are capable. He would have given his whole life to it at the risk of going mad before the year was out. Mad! was he not that already? He had had the idea that the document might be read through the paper, and so he turned it round and exposed it to the light, and tried it in that way.

Nothing! The numbers already thought of, and which he tried in this new way, gave no result. Perhaps the document read backwards, and the last letter was really the first, for the author would have done this had he wished to make the reading more difficult.

Nothing! The new combination only furnished a series of letters just as enigmatic.

At eight o'clock in the evening Jarriquez, with his face in his hands, knocked up, worn out mentally and physically, had neither strength to move, to speak, to think, or to associate one idea with another.

Suddenly a noise was heard outside. Almost immediately, notwithstanding his formal orders, the door of his study was thrown open. Benito and Manoel were before him, Benito looking dreadfully pale, and Manoel supporting him, for the unfortunate young man had hardly strength to support himself.

The magistrate quickly arose.

"What is it, gentlemen? What do you want?" he asked.

"The cipher!—the cipher!" exclaimed Benito, mad with grief—"the cipher of the document."

"Do you know it, then?" shouted the judge.

"No, sir!" said Manoel. "But you?"

"Nothing—nothing!"

"Nothing?" gasped Benito, and in a paroxysm of despair he took a knife from his belt, and would have plunged it into his breast had not the judge and Manoel jumped forward and managed to disarm him.

"Benito," said Jarriquez, in a voice which he tried to keep calm, "if your father cannot escape the expiation of a crime which is not his, you could do something better than kill yourself."

"What?" said Benito.

"Try and save his life!"

"How?"

"That is for you to discover," answered the magistrate, "and not for me to say."

## CHAPTER XVI.

### PREPARATIONS.

ON the following day, the 30th of August, Benito and Manoel talked matters over together. They had understood the thought to which the judge had not dared to give utterance in their presence, and were engaged in devising some means by which the condemned man could escape the penalty of the law.

Nothing else was left for them to do. It was only too certain that for the authorities at Rio Janeiro the undeciphered document would have no value whatever, that it would be a dead letter, that the first verdict which declared Joam Dacosta the perpetrator of the crime at Tijuco would not be set aside, and that, as in such cases no commutation was possible, the order for his execution would inevitably be received.

Once more, then, Joam Dacosta would have to escape by flight from an unjust punishment.

It was at the outset agreed by the two young men that the secret should be carefully kept, and that neither Yaquita nor Minha should be informed of preparations, which would probably only give rise to hopes destined never to be realized. Who could tell if, owing to some unforeseen circumstance, the attempt at escape would not prove a miserable failure?

The presence of Fragoso on such an occasion would have been most valuable. Discreet and devoted, his services would have been most welcome to the two young fellows; but Fragoso had not reappeared. Lina, when asked, could only say that she knew not what had become of him, nor why he had left the raft without telling her anything about it.

And assuredly, had Fragoso foreseen that things would have turned out as they were doing, he would never have left the Dacosta family on an expedition which appeared to promise no serious results. Far better for him to have assisted in the escape of the doomed man than to have hurried of in search of the former comrades of Torres!

But Fragoso was away, and his assistance had to be dispensed with.

At daybreak Benito and Manoel left the raft and proceeded to Manaos. They soon reached the town, and passed through its narrow streets, which at that early hour were quite deserted. In a few minutes they arrived in front of the prison. The waste ground, amid which the old convent which served for a house of detention was built, was traversed by them in all directions, for they had come to study it with the utmost care.

Fifty-five feet from the ground, in an angle of the building, they recognized the window of the cell in which Joam Dacosta was confined. The window was secured with iron bars in a miserable state of repair, which it would be easy to tear down or cut through if they could only get near enough. The badly-jointed stones in the wall, which were crumbled away every here and there, offered many a ledge for the feet to rest on, if only a rope could be fixed to climb up by. One of the bars had slipped out of its socket, and formed a hook over which it might be possible to throw a rope. That done, one or two of the bars could be removed so as to permit a man to get through. Benito and Manoel would then have to make their way into the prisoner's room, and without much difficulty the escape could be managed by means of the rope fastened to the projecting iron. During the night, if the sky were very cloudy, none of these operations would be noticed, and before the day dawned Joam Dacosta could get safely away.

Manoel and Benito spent an hour about the spot, taking care not to attract attention, but examining the locality with great exactness, particularly as regarded the position of the window, the arrangement of the iron bars, and the place from which it would be best to throw the line.

"That is agreed!" said Manoel, at length. "And now, ought Joam Dacosta to be told about this?"

"No, Manoel. Neither to him, any more than to my mother, ought we to impart the secret of an attempt in which there is such a risk of failure."

"We shall succeed, Benito!" continued Manoel. "However, we must prepare for everything; and in case the chief of the prison should discover us at the moment of escape——"

"We shall have money enough to purchase his silence," answered Benito.

"Good!" replied Menoel. "But once your father is out of prison he cannot remain hidden in the town or on the jangada. Where is he to find refuge?"

This was the second question to solve: and a very difficult one it was.

A hundred paces away from the prison, however, the waste land was crossed by one of those canals which flow through the town into the Rio Negro. This canal afforded an easy way of gaining the river if a pirogue were in waiting for the fugitive. From the foot of the wall to the canal side was hardly a hundred yards.

Benito and Manoel decided that about eight o'clock in the evening one of the pirogues, with two strong rowers, under the command of the pilot Araujo, should start from the jangada. They could ascend the Rio Negro, enter the canal, and, crossing the waste land, remain concealed throughout the night under the tall vegetation on the banks.

But once on board, where was Joam Dacosta to seek refuge? To return to Iquitos was to follow a road full of difficulties and peril, and a long one in any case, should the fugitive either travel across the country or by the river. Neither by horse nor pirogue could he be got out of danger quickly enough, and the fazenda was no longer a safe retreat. He would not return to it as the fazender, Joam Garral, but as the

convict, Joam Dacosta, continually in fear of his extradition.   He could never dream of resuming his former
life.

To get away by the Rio Negro into the north of the
province, or even beyond the Brazilian territory,
would require more time than he could spare, and his
first care must be to escape from immediate pursuit.

To start again down the Amazon ?  But stations,
villages, and towns abounded on both sides of the
river.   The description of the fugitive would be sent
to all the police, and he would run the risk of being
arrested long before he reached the Atlantic.   And
supposing he reached the coast, where and how was
he to hide and wait for a passage to put the sea between himself and his pursuers ?

On consideration of these various plans, Benito and
Manoel agreed that neither of them was practicable.
One, however, did offer some chance of safety, and
that was to embark in a pirogue, follow the canal into
the Rio Negro, descend this tributary under the guid-
ance of the pilot, reach the confluence of the rivers,
and run down the Amazon along its right bank for
some sixty miles during the nights, resting during the
daylight, and so gaining the embouchure of the Madeira.

This tributary, which, fed by a hundred affluents,
descends from the waterheads of the Cordilleras, is a
regular waterway opening into the very heart of Bolivia.   A pirogue could pass up it and leave no trace of
his passage, and a refuge could be found in some town
or village beyond the Brazilian frontier.   There Joam
Dacosta would be comparatively safe, and there for
several months he could wait for an opportunity of
reaching the Pacific coast and taking passage in some
vessel leaving one of its ports; and if the ship were
bound for one of the States of North America he
would be free.   Once there, he could sell the fazenda,
leave his country forever, and seek beyond the sea,
in the Old World, a final retreat in which to end an
existence so cruelly and unjustly disturbed.   Anywhere
he might go, his family—not excepting Manoel, who

was bound to him by so many ties—would assuredly follow without the slightest hesitation.

"Let us go," said Benito; "we must have all ready before night, and we have no time to lose."

The young men returned on board by way of the canal bank, which led along the Rio Negro. They satisfied themselves that the passage of the pirogue would be quite possible, and that no obstacles such as locks or boats under repair were there to stop it. They then descended the left bank of the tributary, avoiding the slowly-filling streets of the town, and reached the jangada.

Benito's first care was to see his mother. He felt sufficiently master of himself to dissemble the anxiety which consumed him. He wished to assure her that all hope was not lost, that the mystery of the document would be cleared up, that in any case public opinion was in favor of Joam, and that, in face of the agitation which was being made in his favor, justice would grant all the necessary time for the production of the material proof of his innocence. "Yes, mother," he added, "before to-morrow we shall be free from anxiety."

"May heaven grant it so!" replied Yaquita, and she looked at him so keenly that Benito could hardly meet her glance.

On his part, and as if by pre-arrangement, Manoel had tried to reassure Minha by telling her that Judge Jarriquez was convinced of the innocence of Joam, and would try to save him by every means in his power.

"I only wish he would, Manoel," answered she, endeavoring to restrain her tears.

And Manoel left her, for the tears were also welling up in his eyes and witnessing against the words of hope to which he had just given utterance.

And now the time had arrived for them to make their daily visit to the prisoner, and Yaquita and her daughter set off to Manaos.

For an hour the young men were in consultation with Araujo. They acquainted him with their plan

in all its details, and they discussed not only the pro-
jected escape, but the measures which were necessary
for the safety of the fugitive.

Araujo approved of everything; he undertook,
during the approaching night, to take the pirogue up
the canal without attracting any notice, and he knew
its course thoroughly as far as the spot where he was
to await the arrival of Joam Dacosta. To get back to
the mouth of the Rio Negro was easy enough, and the
pirogue would be able to pass unnoticed among the
numerous craft continually descending the river.

Araujo had no objection to offer to the idea of following the Amazon down to its confluence with the
Madeira. The course of the Madeira was familiar to
him for quite two hundred miles up, and in the midst
of these thinly-peopled provinces, even if pursuit took
place in their direction, all attempts at capture could
be easily frustrated; they could reach the interior of
Bolivia, and if Joam decided to leave his country he
could procure a passage with less danger on the coast
of the Pacific than on that of the Atlantic.

Araujo's approval was most welcome to the young
fellows; they had great faith in the practical good
sense of the pilot, and not without reason. His zeal
was undoubted, and he would assuredly have risked
both life and liberty to save the fazender of Iquitos.

With the utmost secrecy, Araujo at once set about
his preparations. A considerable sum in gold was
handed over to him by Benito to meet all eventualities
during the voyage on the Madeira. In getting the
pirogue ready, he announced his intention of going in
search of Fragoso, whose fate excited a good deal of
anxiety among his companions. He stowed away in
the boat provisions for many days, and did not forget
the ropes and tools which would be required by the
young men when they reached the canal at the appointed time and place.

These preparations evoked no curiosity on the part
of the crew of the jangada, and even the two stalwart
negroes were not let into the secret. They, however,
could be absolutely depended on. Whenever they

learned what the work of safety was in which they
were engaged—when Joam Dacosta, once more free,
was confided to their charge—Araujo knew well that
they would dare anything, even to the risk of their
own lives, to save the life of their master.

By the afternoon all was ready, and they had only
the night to wait for.  But before making a start Manoel wished to call on Judge Jarriquez for the last
time.  The magistrate might perhaps have found out
something new about the document.  Benito preferred
to remain on the raft and wait for the return of his
mother and sister.

Manoel, then, presented himself at the abode of
Judge Jarriquez, and was immediately admitted.

The magistrate, in the study which he never
quitted, was still the victim of the same excitement.
The document, crumpled by his impatient fingers, was
still there, before his eyes, on the table.

"Sir," said Manoel, whose voice trembled as he
asked the question, "have you received anything from
Rio de Janeiro?"

"No," answered the judge; "the order has not yet
come to hand, but it may at any moment."

"And the document?"

"Nothing yet!" exclaimed he.  "Everything my
imagination can suggest I have tried, and no result."

"None?"

"Nevertheless, I distinctly see one word in the
document—only one!"

"What is that—what is the word?"

"'Fly'!"

Manoel said nothing, but he pressed the hand which
Jarriquez held out to him, and returned to the jangada
to wait for the moment of action.

# CHAPTER XVII.

### THE LAST NIGHT.

THE visit of Yaquita and her daughter had been like all such visits during the few hours which each day the husband and wife spent together. In the presence of the two beings whom Joam so dearly loved his heart nearly failed him. But the husband—the father—retained his self-command. It was he who comforted the two poor women and inspired them with a little of the hope of which so little now remained to him. They had come with the intention of cheering the prisoner. Alas! far more than he they themselves were in want of cheering! But when they found him still bearing himself unflinchingly in the midst of his terrible trial, they recovered a little of their hope.

Once more had Joam spoken encouraging words to them. His indomitable energy was due not only to the feeling of his innocence, but to his faith in that God, a portion of whose justice yet dwells in the hearts of men. No! Joam Dacosta would never lose his life for the crime of Tijuco!

Hardly ever did he mention the document. Whether it were apochryphal or no, whether it were in the handwriting of Torres or in that of the real perpetrator of the crime, whether it contained or did not contain the longed-for vindication, it was on no such doubtful hypotheses that Joam Dacosta presumed to trust. No; he reckoned on a better argument in his favor, and it was to his long life of toil and honor that he relegated the task of pleading for him.

This evening, then, his wife and daughter, strengthened by the manly words, which thrilled them to the

core of their hearts, had left him more confident than
they had ever been since his arrest. For the last time
the prisoner had embraced them; and with redoubled
tenderness. It seemed as though he had a presentiment that, whatever it might be, the *denouement* was
nigh.

Joam Dacosta, after they had left, remained for some
time perfectly motionless. His arms rested on a small
table and supported his head. Of what was he thinking? Had he at last been convinced that human justice, after failing the first time, would at length pronounce his acquittal?

Yes, he still hoped. With the report of Judge Jarriquez establishing his identity, he knew that his memoir, which he had penned with so much sincerity,
would have been sent to Rio Janeiro, and was now in
the hands of the Chief Justice. This memoir, as we
know, was the history of his life from his entry into
the offices of the diamond arrayal until the very moment when the jangada stopped before Manaos. Joam
Dacosta was pondering over his whole career. He
again lived his past life from the moment when, as an
orphan, he had set foot in Tijuco. There his zeal had
raised him high in the offices of the governor-general,
into which he had been admitted when still very young.
The future smiled on him; he would have filled some
important position. Then this sudden catastrophe;
the robbery of the diamond convoy, the massacre of
the escort, the suspicion directed against him as the
only official who could have divulged the secret of the
expedition, his arrest, his appearance before the jury,
his conviction in spite of all the efforts of his advocate, the last hours spent in the condemned cell at
Villa Rica, his escape under conditions which betoken-
ed almost superhuman courage, his flight through the
northern provinces, his arrival on the Peruvian frontier, and the reception which the starving fugitive
had met with from the hospitable fazender Magalhaes.

The prisoner once more passed in review these
events, which had so cruelly marred his life. And

then, lost in his thoughts and recollections, he sat, regardless of a peculiar noise on the outer wall of the convent, of the jerkings of a rope hitched on to a bar of his window, and of grating steel as it cut through iron, which ought at once to have attracted the attention of a less absorbed man.

Joam Dacosta continued to live the years of his youth after his arrival in Peru. He again saw the fazender, the clerk, the partner of the old Portuguese, toiling hard for the prosperity of the establishment at Iquitos. Ah! why at the outset had he not told all to his benefactor? He would never have doubted him. It was the only error with which he could reproach himself. Why had he not confessed to him whence he had come, and who he was—above all, at the moment when Magalhaes had placed in his hand the hand of the daughter who would never have believed that he was the author of so frightful a crime.

And now the noise outside became loud enough to attract the prisoner's attention. For an instant Joam raised his head; his eyes sought the window, but with a vacant look, as though he were unconscious, and the next instant his head again sank into his hands. Again he was in thought back at Iquitos.

There the old fazender was dying; before his end he longed for the future of his daughter to be assured, for his partner to be the sole master of the settlement which had grown so prosperous under his management. Should Dacosta have spoken then? Perhaps; but he dared not do it. He again lived the happy days he had spent with Yaquita, and again he thought of the birth of his children, again he felt the happiness which had its only trouble in the remembrances of Tijuco and the remorse that he had not confessed his terrible secret.

The chain of events was reproduced in Joam's mind with a clearness and completeness quite remarkable.

And now he was thinking of the day when his daughter's marriage with Manoel had been decided. Conld he allow that union to take place under a false name without acquainting the lad with the mystery

of his life? No! And so at the advice of Judge
Ribeiro he resolved to come and claim the revision of
his sentence, to demand the rehabilitation which was
his due! He was starting with his people, and then
came the intervention of Torres, the detestable bargain proposed by the scoundrel, the indignant refusal
of the father to hand over his daughter to save his
honor and his life, and then the denunciation and the
arrest?

Suddenly the window flew open with a violent push
from without.

Joam started up; the *souvenirs* of the past vanished
like a shadow.

Benito leaped into the room; he was in the presence
of his father, and the next moment Manoel, tearing
down the remaining bars, appeared before him.

Joam Dacosta would have uttered a cry of surprise.
Benito left him no time to do so.

"Father," he said, "the window grating is down. A
rope leads to the ground. A pirogue is waiting for
you on the canal not a hundred yards off. Araujo is
there ready to take you away from Manaos, on the
other bank of the Amazon, where your track will never
be discovered! Father, you must escape this very
moment! It was the judge's own suggestion!"

"It must be done!" added Manoel.

"Fly! I!—Fly a second time! Escape again?"

And with crossed arms, and head erect, Joam Dacosta stepped backwards.

"Never!" he said, in a voice so firm that Benito and
Manoel stood bewildered.

The young men had never thought of a difficulty
like this. They had never reckoned on the hindrances
to escape coming from the prisoner himself.

Benito advanced to his father, and looking him
straight in the face, and taking both his hands in his,
not to force him, but to try and convince him, said:

"Never, did you say, father?"

"Never!"

"Father," said Manoel—"for I also have the right
to call you father—listen to us! If we tell you that

you ought to fly without losing an instant, it is because if you remain you will be guilty toward others, toward yourself!"

"To remain," continued Benito, "is to remain to die! The order for execution may come at any moment! If you imagine that the justice of men will nullify a wrong decision, if you think it will rehabilitate you whom it condemned twenty years since, you are mistaken! There is hope no longer! You must escape! Come!"

By an irresistible impulse Benito seized his father and drew him towards the window.

Joam Dacosta struggled from his son's grasp and recoiled a second time.

"To fly," he answered, in the tone of a man whose resolution was unalterable, "is to dishonor myself, and you with me! It would be a confession of my guilt! Of my own free will I surrendered myself to my country's judges, and I will await their decision, whatever that decision may be!"

"But the presumptions on which you trusted are insufficient," replied Manoel, "and the material proof of your innocence is still wanting! If we tell you that you ought to fly, it is because Judge Jarriquez himself told us so. You have now only this one chance left to escape from death!"

"I will die, then," said Joam, in a calm voice. "I will die protesting against the decision which condemned me! The first time, a few hours before the execution—I fled! Yes! I was then young. I had all my life before me in which to struggle against man's injustice! But to save myself now, to begin again the miserable existence of a felon hiding under a false name, whose every effort is required to avoid the pursuit of the police, again to live the life of anxiety which I have led for three-and-twenty years, and oblige you to share it with me; to wait each day for a denunciation which sooner or later must come, to wait for the claim for extradition which would follow me to a foreign country! Am I to live for that? No! Never!"

"Father," interrupted Benito, whose mind threatened to give way before such obstinacy, "you shall fly! I will have it so!" And he caught hold of Joam Dacosta, and tried by force to drag him toward the window.

"No! no!"

"You wish to drive me mad!"

"My son," exclaimed Joam Dacosta, "listen to me! Once already I escaped from prison at Villa Rica, and people believed I fled from well-merited punishment. Yes, they had reason to think so. Well, for the honor of the name which you bear I shall not do so again."

Benito had fallen on his knees before his father. He held up his hands to him; he begged him—

"But this order, father," he repeated, "this order, which is due to-day—even now—it will contain your sentence of death."

"The order may come, but my determination will not change. No, my son! Joam Dacosta, guilty, might fly! Joam Dacosta, innocent, will not fly!"

The scene which followed these words was heart-rending. Benito struggled with his father. Manoel, distracted, kept near the window ready to carry off the prisoner—when the door of the room opened.

On the threshold appeared the chief of police, accompanied by the head warder of the prison and a few soldiers. The chief of the police understood at a glance that an attempt at escape was being made; but he also understood from the prisoner's attitude that he it was who had no wish to go! He said nothing. The sincerest pity was depicted on his face. Doubtless he also, like Judge Jarriquez, would have liked Dacosta to have escaped.

It was too late !

The chief of the police, who held a paper in his hand, advanced towards the prisoner.

"Before all of you," said Joam Dacosta, "let me tell you, sir, that it only rested with me to get away and that I would not do so."

The chief of the police bowed his head, and then, in a voice which he vainly tried to control :

"Joam Dacosta," he said, "the order has this moment arrived from the Chief Justice at Rio Janeiro."

"Father!" exclaimed Manoel and Benito.

"This order," asked Joam Dacosta, who had crossed his arms, "this order requires the execution of my sentence?"

"Yes!"

"And that will take place?"

"To-morrow."

Benito threw himself on his father. Again would he have dragged him from his cell, but the soldiers came and drew away the prisoner from his grasp.

At a sign from the chief of the police Benito and Manoel were taken away. An end had to be put to this painful scene, which had already lasted too long.

"Sir," said the doomed man, "before to-morrow, before the hour of my execution, may I pass a few moments with Padre Passanha, whom I ask you to tell?"

"It will be forbidden."

"May I see my family, and embrace for the last time my wife and children?"

"You shall see them."

"Thank you, sir," answered Joam; "and now keep guard over that window: it will not do for them to take me out of here against my will."

And then the chief of the police, after a respectful bow, retired with the warder and the soldiers.

The doomed man, who had but a few hours to live, was left alone.

# CHAPTER XVIII.

## FRAGOSO.

AND so the order had come, and, as Judge Jarriquez had foreseen, it was an order requiring the immediate execution of the sentence pronounced on Joam Dacosta. No proof had been produced ; justice must take its course.

It was the very day—the 31st of August, at nine o'clock in the morning of which the condemned man was to perish on the gallows.

The death penalty in Brazil is generally commuted except in the case of negroes, but this time it was to be suffered by a white man.

Such are the penal arrangements relative to crimes in the diamond arrayal, for which, in the public interest, the law allows no appeal to mercy.

Nothing could now save Joam Dacosta. It was not only life, but honor that he was about to lose.

But on the 31st of August a man was approaching Manaos with all the speed his horse was capable of, and such had been the pace at which he had come, that half a mile from the town, the gallant creature fell, incapable of carrying him any farther.

The rider did not even stop to raise his steed. Evidently he had asked and obtained from it all that was possible, and, despite the state of exhaustion in which he found himself, he rushed off in the direction of the city.

The man came from the eastern provinces, and had followed the left bank of the river. All his means had gone in the purchase of this horse, which, swifter far than any pirogue on the Amazon, had brought him to Manaos.

It was Fragoso !

Had, then, the brave fellow succeeded in the enterprise of which he had spoken to nobody? Had he found the party to which Torres belonged? Had he discovered some secret which would yet save Joam Dacosta?

He hardly knew. But in any case, he was in great haste to acquaint Judge Jarriquez with what he had ascertained during his short journey.

And this is what had happened.

Fragoso had made no mistake when he recognized Torres as one of the captains of the party which was employed in the river provinces of the Madeira.

He set out, and on reaching the mouth of that tributary he learned that the chief of these *capitaes da mato* was then in the neighborhood.

Without losing a minute, Fragoso started on the search, and, not without difficulty, succeeded in meeting him.

To Fragoso's questions the chief of the party had no hesitation in replying ; he had no interest in keeping silence with regard to the few simple matters on which he was interrogated. In fact, three questions only of importance were asked him by Fragoso, and these were:

"Did not a captain of the woods named Torres belong to your party three months ago?"

"Yes."

"At that time had he not one intimate friend among his companions who has recently died?"

"Just so !"

"And the name of that friend was?"

"Ortega."

This was all that Fragoso had learned. Was this information of a kind to modify Dacosta's position? It was hardly likely.

Fragoso saw this, and pressed the chief of the band to tell him what he knew of this Ortega, of the place where he came from, and of his antecedents generally. Such information would have been of great importance if Ortega, as Torres had declared, was the true author of the crime of Tijuco. But unfortunately the chief could give him no information whatever in the matter.

What was certain was that Ortega had been a member of the band for many years, that an intimate friendship existed between him and Torres, that they were always seen together, and that Torres had watched at his bedside when he died.

This was all the chief of the band knew, and he could tell no more. Fragoso, then, had to be contented with these insignificant details, and departed immediately.

But if the devoted fellow had not brought back the proof that Ortega was the author of the crime of Tijuco, he had gained one thing, and that was the knowledge that Torres had told the truth when he affirmed that one of his comrades in the band had died, and that he had been present during his last moments.

The hypothesis that Ortega had given him the document in question had now become admissible. Nothing was more probable than that this document had reference to the crime of which Ortega was really the author, and that it contained the confession of the culprit, accompanied by circumstances which permitted of no doubt as to its truth.

And so, if the document could be read, if the key had been found, if the cipher on which the system hung were known, no doubt of its truth could be entertained.

But this cipher Fragoso did not know. A few more presumptions, a half-certainty that the adventurer had invented nothing, certain circumstances tending to prove that the secret of the matter was contained in the document—and that was all that the gallant fellow brought back from his visit to the chief of the gang of which Torres had been a member.

Nevertheless, little as it was, he was in all haste to relate it to Judge Jarriquez. He knew that he had not an hour to lose, and that was why on this very morning, at about eight o'clock, he arrived, exhausted with fatigue, within half a mile of Manaos. The dis-

tance between there and the town he traversed in a
few minutes. A kind of irresistible presentiment urged
him on, and he had almost come to believe that Joam
Dacosta's safety rested in his hands.

Suddenly Fragoso stopped as if his feet had become
rooted in the ground. He had reached the entrance
to a small square, on to which opened one of the town
gates.

There, in the midst of a dense crowd, arose the gallows, towering up some twenty feet, and from it there
hung the rope!

Fragoso felt his consciousness abandon him. He
fell; his eyes involuntarily closed. He did not wish
to look, and these words escaped his lips : "Too late!
too late!" but by a superhuman effort he raised himself up. No : it was *not* too late, the corpse of Joam
Dacosta was *not* dangling at the end of the rope.

"Judge Jarriquez—Judge Jarriquez!" shouted Fragoso, and, panting and bewildered, he rushed towards
the city gate, dashed up the principal street of Manaos,
and fell, half dead, on the threshold of the judge's
house. The door was shut. Fragoso had still strength
enough left to knock at it.

One of the magistrate's servants came to open it;
his master would see no one.

In spite of this denial, Fragoso pushed back the man
who guarded the entrance, and with a bound threw
himself into the judge's study.

"I come from the province where Torres pursued
his calling as captain of the woods!" he gasped,
"Mr. Judge, Torres told the truth. Stop—stop the
execution!"

"You found the gang?"

"Yes."

"And you have brought me the cipher of the document?"

Fragoso did not reply.

"Come, leave me alone! leave me alone!" shouted
Jarriquez, and, a prey to an outburst of rage, he
grasped the document to tear it to atoms.

Fragoso seized his hands and stopped him. ' The truth is there ! " he said.

"I know," answered Jarriquez ; "but it is a truth which will never see the light ! "

" It will appear—it must ! it must ! "

" Once more, have you the cipher ? "

"No," replied Fragoso ; "but, I repeat, Torres has not lied. One of his companions, with whom he was very intimate, died a few months ago, and there can be no doubt but that this man gave him the document he came to sell to Joam Dacosta."

"No," answered Jarriquez—"no, there is no doubt about it—as far as we are concerned ; but that is not enough for those who dispose of the doomed man's life. Leave me ! "

Fragoso, repulsed, would not quit the spot. Again he threw himself at the judge's feet. " Joam Dacosta is innocent !" he cried ; "you will not leave him to die ? It was not he who committed the crime of Tijuco, it was the comrade of Torres, the author of that document ! It was Ortega !"

As he uttered the name the judge bounded backwards. A kind of calm swiftly succeeded to the tempest which raged within him. He dropped the document from his clenched hand, smoothed it out on the table, sat down, and, passing his hand over his eyes— "That name ?" he said—" Ortega ! Let us see," and then he proceeded with the new name brought back by Fragoso as he had done with the other names so vainly tried by himself.

After placing it above the first six letters of the paragraph, he obtained the following formula :

O r t e g a
*P h y j s l*

" Nothing !" he said. " That gives us—nothing !"

And in fact the *h* placed under the *r* could not be expressed by a cipher, for, in alphabetical order, this letter occupies an earlier position to that of the *r*.

The *p*, the *y*, the *j*, arranged beneath the letters *o, t, e,* disclosed the cipher 1, 4, 5, but as for the *s* and the *l*

at the end of the word, the interval which separated
them from the *g* and the *a* was a dozen letters, and
hence impossible to express by a single cipher, so that
they corresponded to neither *g* nor *a*.

And here appalling shouts arose in the streets ; they
were the cries of despair.

Fragoso jumped to one of the windows, and opened
it before the judge could hinder him.

The people filled the road. The hour had come at
which the doomed man was to start from the prison,
and the crowd was flocking back to the spot where the
gallows had been erected.

Judge Jarriquez, quite frightful to look upon, de-
voured the lines of the document with a fixed stare.

"The last letters!" he muttered. "Let us try once
more the last letters!"

It was the last hope.

And then, with a hand whose agitation nearly prevented him from writing at all, he placed the name of
Ortega over the six last letters of the paragraph, as he
had done over the first.

An exclamation immediately escaped him. He saw,
at first glance, that the six letters were inferior
in alphabetical order to those which composed Ortega's
name, and that consequently they might yield the
number.

And when he reduced the formula, reckoning each
later letter from the earlier letter of the word, he obtained

O r t e g a
4 3 2 5 1 3
*S u v j h d*

The number thus disclosed was 432513.

But was this number that which had been used in
the document? Was it not as erroneous as those he
had previously tried?

At this moment the shouts below redoubled—shouts
of pity which betrayed the sympathy of the excited
crowd. A few minutes more were all that the doomed
man had to live!

Fragoso, maddened with grief, darted from the room. He wished to see, for the last time, his bene-factor who was on his road to death! He longed to throw himself before the mournful procession and stop it, shouting: "Do not kill this just man! do not kill him!"

But already Judge Jarriquez had placed the given number above the first letters of the paragraph, re-peating them as often as was necessary, as follows:

4 3 2 5 1 3 4 3 2 5 1 3 4 3 2 5 1 3 4 3 2 5 1 3
*P h y j s l y d d q f d z x g a s g z z q q e h*

And then, reckoning the true letters according to their alphabetical order, he read:

" *Le veritable auteur du vol de—*"

A yell of delight escaped him! This number, 432513, was the number sought for so long! The name of Ortega had enabled him to discover it! At length he held the key of the document, which would incontestably prove the innocence of Joam Dacosta, and without reading any more he flew from his study into the street, shouting:

"Halt! Halt!"

To cleave the crowd, which opened as he ran, to dash to the prison, whence the convict was coming at the moment, with his wife and children clinging to him with the violence of despair, was but the work of a minute for Judge Jarriquez.

Stopping before Joam Dacosta, he could not speak for a second, and then these words escaped his lips:

"Innocent! Innocent!"

---

## CHAPTER XIX.

### THE CRIME OF TIJUCO.

ON the arrival of the judge the mournful procession halted. A roaring echo had repeated after him and again repeated the cry which escaped from every mouth :

"Innocent! Innocent!"

Then complete silence fell on all. The people did not want to lose one syllable of what was about to be proclaimed.

Judge Jarriquez sat down on a stone seat, and then, while Minha, Benito, Manoel, and Fragoso stood round him, while Joam Dacosta clasped Yaquita to his heart, he first unravelled the last paragraph of the document by means of the number, and as the words appeared by the institution of the true letters for the cryptological ones, he divided and punctuated them, and then read it out in a loud voice. And this is what he read in the midst of profound silence :—

*Le véritable auteur du vol des diamants et de*
4 3 ² 5 1 3 4 3 ² 5 1   3 4 3 ² 5   1 3 4   3 ² 5   1 3 4 3 ² 5 1   3 4
*Ph y j sly ddqf   dz x gas   g z zq q e hx gk f n   drxu   ju   gi*

*l'assassinat des soldats qui escortaient le convoi,*
3 ² 5 1 3 4 3 ² 5 1 3 4 3 ² 5 1 3 4 3 ² 5   1 3 4 3 ² 5   1 3 4 3 ² 5 1 3 4 3 ² 5 1 3 4 3
*o cy t d x vk s bx   hhu   yp   oh dvy   rym huh p uy dk j o x ph e t o z s l*

*commis dans la nuit du vingt-deux janvier mil*
2 5   1 3 4 3   2 5   1 3 4 3   2 5   1 3   4 3   ² 5 1 3 4 3 ² 5 1   3 4 3 ² 5 1 3   4 3 ²
*et np mv f f ov pd p ajx   hy   yn o j y g gay   me q y n fu q l n*

*huit cent vingt-six, n'est donc pas Joam Dacosta,*
5 1 3 4 3 ² 5 1   3 4 3 ² 5   1 3 4   3   ² 5 1   3 4 3 ² 5 1 3 4 3 ² 5   1 3 4 3 ² 5 1
*mvl y fg su zm q iz   t l b   q   gy u g s   qe u bv n rc r   ed gruz b*

*injustement condamné à mort, c'est moi, le misérable*
3 4 3 ² 5 1 3 4 3 ² 5 1 3 4 3 ² 5   1 3 4 3 ² 5 1   3 4 3 ² 5 1 3 4 3 ² 5 1 3 4 3 ² 5 1
*lrmxy u h q hpz   dr rg c r o   h e p qxu f ivv   r p l ph on t hvdd qf*

*employé de l'administration du district diamantin,*
3 4 3 ² 5 1 3 4 3 ² 5 1 3 4 3 ² 5 1 3 4 3 ² 5 1   3 4 3 ² 5 1 3 4 3 ²   5 1 3 4 3 ² 5 1 3
*hq s nt z h hh nfe pmqkyuuexkto g z gk yuumfv   i jdq dpzj q*

*oui, moi seul, qui signe de mon vrai nom, Ortega.*
4 3 ²   5 1 3 4 3 ² 5   1 3 4   3 ² 5 1 3 4 3   ² 5 1   3 4 3 ² 5 1 3   4 3 ² 5 1 3
*sy k   r p l   xhxq   rym vkl oh   hh o t o   zvdk sp p   suvjhd.*

"The real author of the robbery of the diamonds and of the murder of the soldiers who escorted the convoy, committed during the night of the twenty-second of January, one thousand eight hundred and

twenty-six, was thus not Joam Dacosta, unjustly condemned to death; it was I, the wretched servant of the
Administration of the diamond district; yes, I alone,
who sign this with my true name, Ortega. '

The reading of this had hardly finished when the
air was rent with prolonged hurrahs.

What could be more conclusive than this last paragraph, which summarized the whole of the document,
and proclaimed so absolutely the innocence of the
fazender of Iquitos, and which snatched from the gallows this victim of a frightful judicial mistake !

Joam Dacosta surrounded by his wife, his children,
and his friends, was unable to shake the hands which
were held out to him. Such was the strength of his
character, that a reaction occurred, tears of joy escaped
from his eyes, at the same instant his heart was lifted
up to that Providence which had come to save him so
miraculously at the moment he was about to offer the
last expiation to that God who would not permit the
accomplishment of that greatest of crimes, the death
of an innocent man !

Yes ! There could be no doubt as to the vindication of Joam Dacosta. The true author of the crime
of Tijuco confessed of his own free will, and described
the circumstances under which it had been perpe-
trated !

By means of the number Judge Jarriquez inter-
preted the whole of the cryptogram.

And this was what Ortega confessed :

He had been the colleague of Joam Dacosta,
employed, like him, at Tijuco, in the offices of the
governor of the diamond arrayal. He had been the
official appointed to accompany the convoy to Rio de
Janeiro, and, far from recoiling at the horrible idea of
enriching himself by means of murder and robbery,
he had informed the smugglers of the very day the
convoy was to leave Tijuco.

During the attack of the scoundrels, who awaited
the convoy just beyond Villa Rica, he pretended to
defend himself with the soldiers of the escort, and
then, falling among the dead, he was carried away by

his accomplices. Hence it was that the solitary soldier who survived the massacre had reported that
Ortega had perished in the struggle.

But the robbery did not profit the guilty man in the
long run, for, a little time afterwards, he was robbed
by those whom he had helped to commit the crime.

Penniless, and unable to enter Tijuco again, Ortega
fled away to the provinces in the north of Brazil, to
those districts of the Upper Amazon where the *cap-
taes da mato* are to be found. He had to live somehow,
and so he joined this not very honorable company;
they neither asked him who he was nor whence he
came, and so Ortega became a captain of the woods,
and for many years he followed the trade of a chaser
of men.

During this time, Torres, the adventurer, himself in
absolute want, became his companion. Ortega and
he became most intimate. But, as he had told Torres,
remorse began gradually to trouble the scoundrel's
life. The remembrance of his crime became horrible
to him. He knew that another had been condemned
in his place! He knew subsequently that the innocent
man had escaped from the last penalty, but that he
would never be free from the shadow of his capital
sentence! And then, during an expedition of his
party for several months beyond the Peruvian frontier, chance caused Ortega to visit the neighborhood of
Iquitos, and there, in Joam Garral, who did not recognize him, he recognized Joam Dacosta.

Henceforth he resolved to make all the reparation
he could for the injustice of which his old comrade
had been the victim. He committed to the document
all the facts relative to the crime of Tijuco, writing it
first in French, which had been his mother's native
tongue, and then putting it into the mysterious form
we know, his intention being to transmit it to the
fazender of Iquitos, with the cipher by which it could
be read.

Death prevented his completing his work of reparation. Morally wounded in a scuffle with some negroes
on the Madeira, Ortega felt he was doomed. His

comrade Torres was then with him. He thought he could entrust to his friend the secret which had so grievously darkened his life. He gave him the document, and made him swear to convey it to Joam Dacosta, whose name and address he gave him, and with his last breath he whispered the number 432513, without which the document would remain undecipherable.

Ortega dead, we know how the unworthy Torres acquitted himself of his mission, how he resolved to turn to his own profit the secret of which he was the possessor, and how he tried to make it the subject of an odious bargain.

Torres died without accomplishing his work, and carried his secret with him. But the name of Ortega, brought back by Fragoso, and which was the signature of the document, had afforded the means of unravelling the cryptogram, thanks to the sagacity of Judge Jarriquez. Yes, the material proof sought after for so long was the incontestable witness of the innocence of Joam Dacosta, returned to life, restored to honor.

The cheers redoubled when the worthy magistrate, in a loud voice, and for the edification of all, read from the document this terrible history.

And from that moment Judge Jarriquez, who posessed this indubitable proof, arranged with the chief of police, and declined to allow Joam Dacosta, while waiting new instructions from Rio Janeiro, to stay in any prison but his own house.

There could be no difficulty about this, and in the centre of the crowd of the entire population of Manaos, Joam Dacosta, accompanied by all his family, beheld himself conducted like a conqueror to the magistrate's residence.

And in that minute the honest fazender of Iquitos was well repaid for all that he had suffered during the long years of exile, and if he was happy for his family's sake more than for his own, he was none the less proud for his country's sake that this supreme injustice had not been consummated !

And in all this what had become of Fragoso?

Well, the good-hearted fellow was covered with ca-
resses !  Benito, Manoel, and Minha, had overwehlmed
him, and Lina had by no means spared him.  He did
not know what to do, he defended himself as best he
could.  He did not deserve anything like it.  Chance
alone had done it.  Were any thanks due to him for
having recognized Torres as the captain of the woods?
No, certainly not.  As for his idea of  hurrying off in
search of the band to which Torres belonged, he did
not think it had been worth much, and as to the name
of Ortega, he did not even know its value.

Gallant Fragoso !  Whether he wished it  or not he
had none the less saved Joam Dacosta !

And herein what a strange succession of different
events all tending to the same end.  The deliverance
of Fragoso at the time he was dying of exhaustion in
the forest of Iquitos ; the hospitable reception he had
met with at the fazenda, the meeting with Torres on
the Brazilian frontier, his embarkation on the jangada;
aud lastly, the fact that Fragoso had seen him somewhere before.

"Well,  yes !" Fragoso ended  by exelaiming ;  "but
it is not to me that all this happiness is  due, it is due
to Lina !"

"To me ?" replied the young mulatto.

"No doubt of it.  Without the liana, without the
idea of the liana, could I ever have been the cause of
so much happiness ?"

So that Fragoso and Lina were  praised and petted
by all the family, and by all  the new friends whom so
many trials had procured them at Manaos, need hardly be insisted on.

But had not Judge Jarriquez also had  his share in
this rehabilitation of an innocent man?  If, in spite of
all the shrewdness of his analytical talents, he had not
been able to read the document, which was absolutely
undecipherable to any one who had  not got the key,
had he not at any rate discovered the system on which
the cryptogram was composed?  Without him what
could have been done with only the name of Ortega to
reconstruct  the  number  which the  author of  the

crime and Torres, both of whom were dead, alone knew?

And so he also received abundant thanks.

Needless to say that the same day there was sent to Rio de Janeiro a detailed report of the whole affair, and with it the original document and the cipher to enable it to be read. New instructions from the Minister of Justice had to be waited for, though there could be no doubt that they would order the immediate discharge of the prisoner. A few days would thus have to be passed at Manaos, and then Joam Dacosta and his people, free from all constraint, and released from all apprehension, would take leave of their host to go on board once more and continue their descent of the Amazon to Para, where the voyage was intended to terminate with the double marriage of Minha and Manoel and Lina and Fragoso.

Four days afterward, on the fourth of September, the order of discharge arrived. The document had been recognized as authentic. The handwriting was really that of Ortega, who had been formerly employed in the diamond district, and there could be no doubt that the confession of his crime, with the minutest details that were given, had been written entirely with his own hand.

The innocence of the convict of Villa Rica was at length admitted. The rehabilitation of Joam Dacosta was at last officially proclaimed.

That very day Judge Jarriquez dined with the family on board the giant raft, and when evening came he shook hands with them all. Touching were the adieus, but an engagement was made for them to see him again on their return at Manaos, and later on at the fazenda of Iquitos.

On the morning of the morrow, the 5th of September, the signal for departure was given. Joam Dacosta and Yaquita, with their daughter and sons, were on the deck of the enormous raft. The jangada had its moorings slackened off and began to move with the current, and when it disappeared round the bend of the Rio Negro, the hurrahs of the whole pop-

ulaton of Manaos, who were assembled on the bank,
again and again re-echoed across the stream.

## CHAPTER XX.

### THE LOWER AMAZON.

LITTLE remains to tell of the second part of the
voyage down the mighty river. It was but a series of days of joy. Joam Dacosta returned to a new
life, which shed its happiness on all who belonged to
him.

The giant raft glided along with greater rapidity on
the waters now swollen by the floods. On the left they
passed the small village of Don Jose de Maturi, and on
the right the mouth of that Madeira which owes its
name to the floating masses of vegetable remains and
trunks denuded of their foliage which it bears from
the depths of Bolivia. They passed the archipelago
of Caniny, whose islets are veritable boxes of palms,
and before the village of Serpa, which, successively
transported from one bank to the other, has definitely
settled on the left side of the river, with its little
houses, whose thresholds stand on the yellow carpet
of the beach.

The village of Silves, built on the left of the Amazon, and the town of Villa Bella, which is the principal guarana market in the whole province, were soon
left behind by the giant raft. And so was the village
of Faro and its celebrated river of thc Nhamundas,
on which, in 1539, Orellana asserted he was attacked
by female warriors, who have never been seen again
since, and thus gave us the legend which justifies
the immortal name of the river of the Amazons.

Here it is that the province of Rio Negro termin-
ates. The jurisdiction of Para then commences ; and
on the 22d of September the family, marvelling much
at a valley which has no equal in the world, entered

that portion of the Brazilian empire which has no boundary to the east except the Atlantic.

" How magnificent !" remarked Minha, over and over again.

" How long !" murmured Manoel.

" How beautiful ! " repeated Lina.

" When shall we get there ?" murmured Fragoso.

And this was what might have been expected of these folks from their different points of view, though time passed pleasantly enough with them all the same. Benito, who was neither patient nor impatient, had recovered all his former good humor.

Soon the jangada glided between interminable plantations of cocoa-trees, with their sombre green flanked by the yellow thatch or ruddy tiles of the roofs of the huts of the settlers on both banks from Chidos up to the town of Monte Alegre.

Then there opened out the mouth of the Rio Trombetas, bathing with its black waters the houses of Obidos, situated at about one hundred and eighty miles from Belem, quite a small town, and even a "citade " with large streets bordered with handsome habitations, and a great centre for cocoa produce. Then they saw another tributary, the Tapajoz, with its greenish-grey waters descending from the southwest; and then Santarem, a wealthy town of not less than five thousand inhabitants, Indians for the most part, whose nearest houses were built on the vast beach of white sand.

After its departure from Manaos the jangada did not stop anywhere as it passed down the much less encumbered course of the Amazon. Day and night it moved along under the vigilant care of its trusty pilot; no more stoppages either for the gratification of the passengers or for business purposes. Unceasingly it progressed, and the end rapidly grew nearer.

On leaving Alemquer, situated on the left bank, a new horizon appeared in view. In place of the curtain of forests which had shut them in up to then, our friends beheld a foreground of hills, whose undulations could be easily described, and beyond them the

faint summits of veritable mountains vandyked across
the distant path of sky. Neither Yaquita, nor her
daughter, nor Lina, nor old Cybele, had ever seen anything like this.

But in this jurisdiction of Para Manoel was at home,
and he could tell them the names of the double chain
which gradually narrowed the valley of the huge river.

"To the right," said he, "that is the Sierra de Para-
cuarta, which curves in a half circle to the south! To
the left, that is the Sierra de Curuva, of which we have
already passed the first outposts."

"Then they close in?" asked Fragoso.

"They close in!" replied Manoel.

And the two young men seemed to understand each
other, for the same slight but significant nodding of
the head accompanied the question and reply.

At last, notwithstanding the tide, which since leaving Obidos had begun to be felt, and which somewhat
checked the progress of the raft, the town of Monte
Alegre was passed, then that of Pravnha de Onteiro,
then the mouth of the Xingu, frequented by Yurumas
Indians, whose principal industry consists in preparing
their enemies' heads for natural history cabinets.

To what a superb size the Amazon had now devel-
oped, as already this monarch of rivers gave signs of
opening out like a sea! Plants from eight to ten feet
high clustered along the beach, and bordered it with
a forest of reeds. Porto de Mos, Boa Vista, and Gu-
rupa, whose prosperity is on the decline, were soon
among the places left in the rear.

Then the river divided into two important branches,
which flowed off toward the Atlantic, one going away
northeastward, the other eastward, and between them
appeared the beginning of the large Island of Marajo.
This island is quite a province in itself. It measures
no less than a hundred and eighty leagues in circumfer-
ence. Cut up by marshes and rivers, all savannah to
the east, all forest to the west, it offers most excellent
advantages for the raising of cattle, which can here be
seen in their thousands. This immense barricade of
Marajo is the natural obstacle which has compelled

the Amazon to divide before precipitating its torrents
of water into the sea. Following the upper branch,
the jangada, after passing the islands of Caviana and
Mexiana, would have found an embouchure of some
fifty leagues across, but it would also have met with a
bar of the prororoca, that terrible eddy which, for the
three days preceding the new or full moon, takes but
two minutes instead of six hours to raise the river
from twelve to fifteen feet above ordinary high-water
mark.

This is by far the most formidable of tide-races.
Most fortunately the lower branch, known as the Canal
of Breves, which is the natural arm of the Para, is not
subject to the visitations of this terrible phenomenon,
and its tides are of a more regular description. Araujo,
the pilot, was quite aware of this. He steered, therefore, into the midst of magnificent forests, here and
there gliding past islands covered with muritis palms;
and the weather was so favorable that they did not
experience any of the storms which so frequently rage
along this Breves Canal.

A few days afterward the jangada passed the village
of the same name, which, although built on ground
flooded for many months in the year, has become,
since 1845, an important town of a hundred houses.
Throughout these districts, which are frequented by
Tapuyas, the Indians of the Lower Amazon become
more and more commingled with the white population, and promise to be completely absorbed by them.

And still the jangada continued its journey down
the river. Here, at the risk of entanglement, it graz-
ed the branches of the mangliers, whose roots stretched down into the waters like the claws of gigantic
crustaceans; then the smooth trunks of the paletu-
viers, with their pale green foliage, served as the rest-
ing-places for the long poles of the crew as they kept
the raft in the strength of the current.

Then came the Tocantins, whose waters, due to the
different rivers of the province of Goyaz, mingle with
those of the Amazon by an embouchure of great size,
then the Moju, then the town of Santa Ana.

Majestically the panorama of both banks moved along without a pause, as though some ingenious mechanism necessitated its unrolling in the opposite direction to that of the stream.

Already numerous vessels descending the river, ubas, egariteas, vigilindas, pirogues of all builds, and small coasters from the lower districts of the Amazon and the Atlantic seaboard, formed a procession with the giant raft, and seemed like sloops beside some mighty man-of-war.

At length there appeared on the left Santa Maria de Belem do Para—the "town," as they call it in that country—with its picturesque lines of white houses at many different levels, its convents nestled among the palm-trees, the steeples of its cathedral and of Nostra Senora de Merced, and the flotilla of its brigantines, brigs and barques, which form its commercial communications with the old world.

The hearts of the passengers of the giant raft beat high. At length they were coming to the end of the voyage which they had thought they would never reach. While the arrest of Joam detained them at Manaos, half way on their journey, could they ever have hoped to see the capital of the province of Para?

It was in the course of this day, the 15th of October —four months and a half after leaving the fazenda of Iquitos—that, as they rounded a sharp bend in the river, Belem came in sight.

The arrival of the jangada had been signalled for some days. The whole town knew the story of Joam Dacosta. They came forth to welcome him, and to him and his people accorded a most sympathetic reception.

Hundreds of craft of all sorts conveyed them to the fazenda, and soon the jangada was invaded by all those who wished to welcome the return of their compatriot after his long exile. Thousands of sight-seers —or more exactly speaking, thousands of friends— crowded on to the floating village as soon as it came to its moorings, and it was vast and solid enough to support the entire population. Among those who hurried on board one of the first pirogues had brought Madame Valdez. Manoel's mother was at last able to clasp to her arms the daughter whom her son had chosen. If the good lady had not been able to come to Iquitos, was it not as though a portion of the fazenda, with her new family, had come down the Amazon to her?

Before evening the pilot Araujo had securely moored the raft at the entrance of a creek behind the arsenal. That was to be its last resting-place, its last halt, after its voyage of eight hundred leagues on the great Brazilian artery. There the huts of the Indians, the cottages of the negroes, the storerooms which held the valuable cargo, would be gradually demolished; there the principal dwelling, nestled beneath its verdant tapestry of flowers and foliage, and the little chapel whose humble bell was then replying to the sounding clangor from the steeples of Belem, would each in its turn disappear.

But, ere this was done, a ceremony had to take place on the jangada—the marriage of Manoel and Minha, the marriage of Lina and Fragoso. To Father Passanha fell the duty of celebrating the double union which promised so happily. In that little chapel the two couples were to receive the nuptial benediction from his hands.

If it happened to be so small as to be only capable of holding the members of Dacosta's family, was not the giant raft large enough to receive all those who wished to assist at the ceremony? and if not, and the crowd became so great, did not the ledges of the river banks afford sufficient room for as many others of the sympathizing crowd as were desirous of welcoming him whom so signal a reparation had made the hero of the day?

It was on the morrow, the 16th of October, that, with great pomp, the marriages were celebrated.

It was a magnificent day, and from about ten o'clock in the morning the raft began to receive its crowds of guests. On the bank could be seen almost the entire population of Belem in holiday costume. On the

river, vessels of all sorts crammed with visitors, gath-
ered round the enormous mass of timber, and the
waters of the Amazon literally disappeared, even up
to the left bank, beneath the vast flotilla.

When the chapel bell rang out its opening note it
seemed like a signal of joy to ear and eye. In an instant the churches of Belem replied to the bell of the
jangada. The vessels in the port decked themselves
with flags up to their mastheads, and the Brazilian
colors were saluted by the. many other national flags.
Discharges of musketry reverberated on all sides, and
it was only with difficulty that their joyous detona-
tions could cope with the loud hurrahs from the assembled thousands.

The Dacosta family came forth from their house
and moved through the crowd toward the little chapel.
Joam was received with absolutely frantic applause.
He gave his arm to Madame Valdez; Yaquita was
escorted by the Governor of Belem, who, accompanied
by the friends of the young army surgeon, had expressed a wish to honor the ceremony with his presence. Manoel walked by the side of Minha, who looked most fascinating in her bride's costume, and then
came Fragoso, holding the hand of Lina, who seemed
quite radiant with joy. Then followed Benito, then
old Cybele and the servants of the worthy family between the double ranks of the crew of the jangada.

Padre Passanha awaited the two couples at the entrance of the chapel. The ceremony was very simple,
and the same hands which had formerly blessed Joam
and Yaquita were again stretched forth to give the
nuptial benediction to their child.

So much happiness was not likely to be interrupted
by the sorrow of long separation. In fact, Manoel
Valdez almost immediately sent in his resignation,
so as to join the family at Iquitos, where he is still
following his profession as a country doctor.

Naturally the Fragosos did not hesitate to go back
with those who were to them friends rather than masters.

Madame Valdez had no desire to separate so happy

a group, but she insisted on one thing, and that was that they should often come and see her at Belem. Nothing could be easier. Was not the mighty river a bond of communication between Belem and Iquitos? In a few days the first mail steamer was to begin a regular and rapid service, and it would then only take a week to ascend the Amazon, on which it had taken the giant raft so many months to drift. The important commercial negotiations, ably managed by Benito, were carried through under the best conditions, and soon of what had formed this jangada—that is to say, the huge raft of timber constructed from an entire forest at Iquitos—there remained not a trace.

A month afterwards the fazender, his wife, his son, Manoel and Minha Valdez, Lina and Fragoso, departed by one of the Amazon steamers for the immense establishment at Iquitos of which Benito was to take the management.

Joam Dacosta re-entered his home with his head erect, and it was indeed a family of happy hearts which he brought back with him from beyond the Brazilian frontier. As for Fragoso, twenty times a day at least was he heard to repeat: "What! without the liana?" and he wound up by bestowing the name on the young mulatto who, by her affection for the gallant fellow fully justified its appropriateness. "If it were not for the one letter," he said, "would not Lina and Liana be the same?"

THE END.